GALAXY'S EDGE
EDITED BY MIKE RESNICK

ISSUE 32: May 2018

Mike Resnick, Editor
Taylor Morris, Copyeditor
Shahid Mahmud, Publisher

Published by Arc Manor/Phoenix Pick
P.O. Box 10339
Rockville, MD 20849-0339

Galaxy's Edge is published in January, March, May, July,
September, and November.

Please refer to our web-site for submission guidelines.

All material is either copyright © 2017 by Arc Manor LLC,
Rockville, MD, or copyright © by the respective authors as
indicated within the magazine. All rights reserved.

This magazine (or any portion of it) may not be copied or
reproduced, in whole or in part, by any means, electronic,
mechanical or otherwise, without written permission from the
publisher, except by a reviewer who may quote brief passages
in a review.

ISBN: 978-1-61242-410-1

SUBSCRIPTION INFORMATION:
Paper and digital subscriptions are available (including via
Amazon.com) . Please visit our home page: www.GalaxysEdge.
com

ADVERTISING:
Advertising is available in all editions of the magazine. Contact
advert@GalaxysEdge.com.

FOREIGN LANGUAGE RIGHTS:
Refer all inquiries pertaining to foreign language rights to
Shahid Mahmud, Arc Manor, P.O. Box 10339, Rockville, MD
20849-0339. Tel: 1-240-645-2214. Fax 1-310-388-8440. Email
admin@ArcManor.com.

CONTENTS

FRIDAY
ROBERT A. HEINLEIN

HUGO AND NEBULA NOMINATED NOVEL

Now available as an ebook

THE EDITOR'S WORD

by Mike Resnick

Welcome to the thirty-second issue of *Galaxy's Edge*.

We're happy to bring you some new and newer writers, including Effie Seiberg, Laurence Raphael Brothers, Karlo Yeager Rodriguez, Walter Dinjos, Leah Cypess, Brian K. Lowe, Brian Trent, and Alex Shvartsman, plus old friends Joe Haldeman, Kij Johnson, Kristine Kathryn Rusch, Barry N. Malzberg, and Gardner Dozois, and book recommendations by Bill Fawcett and Jody Lynn Nye, a science column by Gregory Benford, a literature column by Robert J. Sawyer, the Joy Ward interview with Catherine Asaro, and another installment of Joan Slonczewski's *Daughter of Elysium*.

In other words, it's a typical issue of *Galaxy's Edge*.

☼

Last issue's editorial discussed the couple of dozen superstars currently working in the field who are all in their 70s and 80s.

It's not *that* unusual. If there are more now than thirty or sixty years ago, it's because the field is larger now, and medicine is better now.

Sooner or later, though, we all die. And conventions are quick to note our passing and to honor our memories. I've been to some fascinating, informative, and moving memorial panels in honor of Isaac Asimov, Robert A. Heinlein, E. E. "Doc" Smith, A. E. van Vogt, and a number of others.

But one writer whose memorial panel I never attended was Jack Williamson, a close personal friend, and a man who was widely considered the Dean of Science Fiction during the final three decades of his life.

And do you know why I never attended it?

Because they never had it.

In a stroke of genius that has yet to be emulated, Noreascon Four, the 2004 Worldcon, didn't wait for Jack to die.

He was in his mid-90s, and had not been up to traveling to distant conventions—he lived in New Mexico, Noreascon was in Boston—for a couple of years, but he was still alive, still writing, still in possession of his senses, and still in possession of a telephone.

So Noreascon put together a Jack Williamson appreciation panel. I was asked to chair it, and the participants included Eleanor Wood, Jack's agent; Fred Pohl, Jack's major collaborator; Stanley Schmidt, Dave Hartwell, Jim Frenkel and Scott Edelman, four of Jack's editors; and Connie Willis, Michael Swanwick, Larry Niven, and Jack Chalker, Jack's long-time friends.

And Jack wasn't merely a distant observer. We phoned him at a pre-arranged time a few minutes before the panel started, and tied the phone into the speaker system so that he could hear every word that was said and the entire audience could hear his response.

I think that kind of tribute is both more enjoyable and more enlightening than the posthumous type. I'm not saying that we should eliminate the latter, but rather that all these years after the Williamson example, conventions should realize that there is no need to wait for each of us to die before following Noreascon's example.

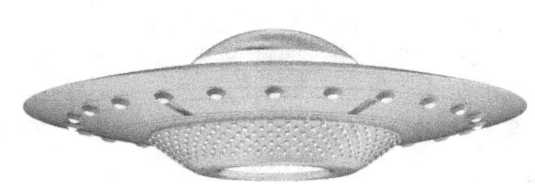

Effie Seiberg's recent short fiction can be found in Analog, *PodCastle, and* Escape Pod. *This is her fourth appearance in* Galaxy's Edge.

JUST ONE MORE KITTEN GIF

by Effie Seiberg

Jen's final sociology paper was due tomorrow, so naturally she was procrastinating online. She hadn't gotten out of bed, much less her dorm, for the past six hours. Her Reddit links were all purple, and Instagram and Tumblr were beginning to repeat themselves. The paper just seemed so daunting, and was worth half her grade...so yeah, no pressure.

"Just one more kitten GIF, then back to work," she thought, and clicked. A sudden whirling vortex of pungent black smoke emerged from nothingness to engulf her.

She found herself transported to a plain gray office, still barefoot in her monkey-print pajamas and holding her laptop. Sitting at a dull wooden desk was a red demon in a tie, engrossed in a pile of yellowed paperwork and occasionally clicking an abacus. He looked like a bodybuilder, if said bodybuilder was red and horned, and was stuck in an uncomfortable office job from two hundred years ago. His nameplate said "Uz". He stamped the top page with a wet thud and turned to a stunned Jen.

"OK, let's see, you're Jen Sanchez, correct?" Without waiting for an answer, he continued. "You've logged more hours of procrastination than anyone else in your school so far this year. Very impressive."

Jen gaped at him. "What...where am I?"

Uz turned his attention back to his papers. "Procrastination Limbo. We're in the administrative wing of the temple of the demon UR. I'm processing you." Thud, thud, went the stamp.

"Processing me? For what?"

"You're being upgraded to Acolyte."

"Wait, *what?*" This must be a dream. Jen gripped her laptop, which was still warm. Crap. Things don't feel warm in dreams.

Uz sighed. "The great demon UR draws his power from wasted minds, tapping in and using the idle components for his own purposes. Our initial operation focused on daydreaming, but we try to keep up

with new improvements. We're very excited about this internet thing."

"A demon's been using my mind?" Clearly her schoolwork wasn't getting the brain space.

"Your mind and everybody else's. Of course, when we have a gifted procrastinator like yourself, we bring them in to better serve the demon UR. Congratulations."

For the tiniest second, this felt like a relief. Endless procrastination instead of her paper? DONE. But Jen dismissed the thought as soon as it came in. *OF COURSE* that wasn't an option. She needed to get out of here.

Uz handed Jen a stack of paperwork. "I'll take you to Medical for brain prep."

New plan: she needed to get out of here *FAST*. Barefoot and armed with nothing but a laptop seemed a bad start. Anything to stall for time would be helpful. "What happens there?"

"A priest lulls your brain into a permanent state of passivity, then you do what you've been doing—waste time online. Optimizes the intake for UR. Eventually you'll become a full priest, worshipping for all eternity."

"So, what if I don't *want*—"

The demon gave her a pointed look.

"Um, to do this without my fuzzy slippers? So if I can just go back to my dorm and grab them—"

"You'll have everything you need here." He reached out from under the desk and snapped a cold metal manacle on her wrist, then grabbed the end of its chain. "Now, if you'll follow me..."

She stumbled down a maze of whitewashed corridors behind the demon. Both he and the chain were too strong to fight, and even if she could there was no clear direction to run—just rooms and rooms of zombie-eyed people chained to laptops, lava lamps, and tables with Mahjong tiles and solitaire cards and something that involved a lot of tiny knots of string. Crap. That didn't look reversible. Time to stall, get information, *something*...

"So UR is all about the internet now, huh?" They kept walking through the endless maze.

"Oh no," said the demon with pride. "We don't bother UR with the details, especially as these things are so flash-in-the-pan. Our operation runs so smoothly that he hasn't needed to check up on us in three hundred years. Lets him focus on the enslavement of humanity. Very dedicated. Even goes up to Earth once a week to check on things."

There was a way out, and it was through UR.

"Can I meet him?"

"Why would you want to do that?"

"Um…I'd like to thank him for this amazing opportunity. Gosh do I love the internet. And procrastinating. Uh…and also of course UR himself."

The demon considered for a moment, looked at the chain still holding her, then shrugged. "I don't see why not. I can take you there after Medical."

"But wouldn't it be better before? Now, I could probably express my gratitude better. He's surrounded by passive people who can't really show their passion for the project."

Uz hesitated.

"I mean, I bet he *never* feels appreciated for what he does. You'd be the first demon to really give him that acknowledgement from an Acolyte!"

Please buy this bullshit please buy this bullshit. The bubble of panic was welling in her chest.

"…Fine. But no funny business." Uz gave the chain a pointed tug.

He led her back through the maze to a huge white domed chamber where an enormous demon, easily the size of a small apartment, sat cross-legged. UR's golden skin glowed against the curved white walls—a demonic yolk in an egg. He seemed to be meditating, with eyes closed and face serene.

On the other side of the room were doors labeled *Supplies*, *Cafeteria*, and most importantly, *Earth*.

Jen's guide coughed politely, and UR opened his eyes. "Who dares disturb my work?" His voice echoed over the chamber.

"It is I, Uz, your servant." Uz bowed. "I come bearing an Acolyte who wishes to worship you directly and give gratitude."

UR sighed. "Very well. But be quick. I'm busy."

Jen stepped forward, still tethered to Uz. The chain stopped her from going further and she gave it a light but pointed tug. Uz sighed and walked over with her. She stood next to UR's crossed legs, his knee a good four feet over the top of her head.

"Oh great demon UR, I thank you for this amazing opportunity."

"Uh huh." The demon looked bored.

Jen opened her laptop, which automatically connected to LimboWiFi. "Great demon UR, I wish to share some of the ecstasy you've allowed me to feel. By your grace, I've been mildly entertained for hours." It was another long shot. There was no way the demon could see anything on a screen that small.

Uz looked uncomfortable. This probably made him look bad next to his boss. Good. "Your Grace, this will be more efficient if you were to adjust for sizing…if you should so wish…"

"If that will make this go faster," rumbled UR. He shrank down to merely twice Jen's height. Still an imposing presence.

She moved closer and opened up a video of a skateboarder face-planting onto a railing. No response from UR, who still looked bored. Jen tried again, and showed a Vine of a teenager coughing up a tablespoon of cinnamon.

UR tapped his claws. "Are you done?"

Jen gulped, and in a last-ditch effort, opened a video of a sneezing panda. A grin cracked UR's face. Really? Cute things did the trick? So Jen followed this with a GIF of otters holding hands, and the demon's smile widened. He grabbed the laptop with a gargantuan hand and began clicking in earnest. Monkeys hugging puppies, piglets wearing boots, penguins slipping on ice.

Uz coughed nervously. "Sir, perhaps it is time to get back to work…" He reached for the laptop, letting go of the chain.

With both demons distracted, Jen sprinted toward the door labeled *Earth*, bare feet slapping the floor and chain jingling behind her, with the first sentences of her new sociology paper on addictive behaviors in internet forums forming in her head. As she passed through the door, a voice boomed behind her. "Yeah. Just a sec. Just one more kitten GIF."

Copyright © 2018 by Effie Seiberg

Alex Shvartsman has been making a name for himself as a writer, an anthology editor (for Baen Books and his own company), and a publisher (as UFO Publishing he has published the Unidentified Funny Objects series as well as other humorous anthologies, most recently The Cackle of Cthulhu*).*

DIAMONDS IN THE ROUGH

by Alex Shvartsman

"I'm going out, Mom," Igor called out from his room. He grabbed a leather jacket, then retrieved the shoebox he kept atop the wardrobe where his younger siblings couldn't reach.

"Dinner is almost ready, Igor," his mother shouted back from the kitchen over the sound of the radio. "Can you wait?"

"Can't, Mom. It's work." Cheap posters of Hollywood action stars stared at him from where they were affixed to the fading wallpaper. Igor opened the box and took out an old police-issue Makarov pistol.

His boss, whose last name was also Makarov, had laughed when he'd given it to him. "This is the official handgun for anyone in my crew. No Nagants or Tokarevs, not for my men." This Makarov had no connection to his namesake gun designer from the '40s, but he acted as though the ongoing popularity of this model fifty years later was somehow his personal accomplishment.

Igor checked the pistol and put it into the inner pocket of his jacket. Although he never fired it outside of the shooting range, it made him feel like the badass heroes from the foreign films, the ones who could walk away from explosions and mayhem behind them without flinching or looking back.

"Keep out of trouble." His mother's cracking voice betrayed her apprehension.

Neither of them liked the idea of him working for Makarov, but he had little choice. Ever since Gorbachev let loose with this Perestroika business, the country was coming apart at the seams. With no government funds coming in, the newly privatized factories had cut their staff. Igor's father was laid off and couldn't find steady work. Hyperinflation wiped out whatever meager savings his family had. The

money seventeen-year-old Igor was able to bring in was indispensible to their family's survival.

A brand-new 1990 Mercedes-Benz 600 was parked halfway on the sidewalk in front of the building. It was painted a garish shade of dark purple, clearly an aftermarket job.

Makarov was one of the New Russians, a small group of opportunists who'd found a way to grow rich by appropriating the crumbling bits of the Soviet empire. Among the New Russians it was not merely acceptable but expected to flaunt their wealth, and Makarov was no exception. In the city where unemployment soared toward fifty percent, his fleet of purple foreign cars paraded his opulence.

Igor climbed in the back.

"You're late," said Sharik without turning.

The driver was a grim older man. No one knew his real name save for, perhaps, Makarov himself. To everyone else he was just Sharik, and he didn't seem to mind being called by a common dog's name. He wore a sleeveless shirt displaying heavily tattooed forearms which told the story of years spent within the Russian penal system.

"I'm right on time. You're early," Igor snapped back, then turned to the man in the front passenger seat. "Hello, Leonid Nikolayevich."

"Hello, Igor," said the geologist.

They rode in silence for a time. Leonid looked more fidgety than usual, chewing his lower lip. "This is a bad idea," he told Sharik. "I don't think Mak should be double-crossing those Chechens. They're bandits, not businessmen. They don't play nice."

"Shut up, four-eyes," said Sharik. "You're not paid to think. Besides, this is not something you should be yapping about in front of the kid."

Igor frowned. He knew what Makarov was up to. He was young, not stupid. Sharik didn't trust him, but then Sharik didn't trust anyone except for the boss, as best as he could tell.

They rode the rest of the way in silence and arrived at a warehouse on the outskirts of the city, where several armed guards were posted at the entrance. Sharik dropped him and the geologist off, waved to the guards, and left on another errand.

The large industrial building was mostly empty, with only a handful of wooden crates stacked by one of the walls. A few stools were placed near the crates.

Makarov and a group of his men sat there. Another stool housed several glasses and a half-empty bottle of vodka.

Makarov was telling some kind of a raunchy joke. He raised his glass in greeting, the clear liquid sloshing inside. His hand was steady and he didn't slur his words, which meant he had kept his drinking to a minimum.

"Good evening, Mak." Igor knew his employer preferred to be called by his nickname.

Makarov wore a bright-red jacket over a yellow T-shirt and black jeans. A thick gold chain hung around his neck and a large Rolex gleamed on his arm. On his face was a self-satisfied smirk of a man who was denied nothing, and he carried himself with the swagger of a 1920s gangster from an American movie. Igor thought that Makarov couldn't act or look any more a stereotype of a New Russian if he tried.

"My customers will be here soon. For now, relax, have a drink or two. Just not so many that it will affect your skills, eh, Leonid?" Makarov chuckled and filled their glasses.

After imbibing some liquid courage, Leonid spoke up. "This isn't right, boss. We have a good thing going with the Chechens. Why rock the boat?"

Makarov looked his underling up and down. "This is business," he said. "The Chechens aren't our friends, they aren't our family. They're just customers, and they were outbid."

"But when you made the deal with the Chechens you said you wanted to sell them the guns because they'd take them far away from here." The geologist gesticulated as he talked. "Who knows what these new people might do?"

Igor agreed with Leonid's sentiment, but he was smart enough to keep his mouth shut.

Selling weapons was a recent thing, but not entirely unexpected. Makarov earned enormous profits by selling off whatever he could get his hands on to anyone who would pay: heavy machinery from the now-shuttered factories, reams of copper wiring meant for maintaining the city infrastructure, even Soviet-era statues of Lenin that foreign collectors wanted for some reason. All of these things belonged to the Russian people, but in the post-Soviet chaos there was no strong government, no police force with authority and will to stop the profiteers. As things deteriorated, it became possible for Makarov to pilfer even military supplies, and he jumped at the opportunity.

Igor figured Makarov would blow up at Leonid for his questions, but the boss was in a good mood.

"The Chechens are crazy and they're still in our backyard, not so far away," said Makarov. "But these new people, they'll export the guns to Africa or South America, to some nasty little war in a place you can't even find on the map. And they'll pay extra for the privilege. Blood diamonds they can't easily move in Europe, so we get them at a discount rate. Once you examine them, of course." He saluted Leonid with his glass. "It's a win-win. You see that now?"

Leonid nodded reluctantly. "Yes, Mak."

"Good." Makarov grinned. "Stick with me, boys, and I'll keep you in vodka. I've got plans for us, big plans." He drained the rest of his glass.

Makarov's business associates showed up fifteen minutes later. There were two of them, a man and a woman, dressed in nearly identical black business suits. The man carried a shoulder bag.

Something was strange about the pair, though Igor couldn't quite put his finger on it. They walked and carried themselves in a slightly odd way. Their facial features were exotic: round eyes that were just a little too large, ruddy complexions, weak chins, and short earlobes. Igor wondered where they were from, wondered if Makarov knew, or cared.

Makarov and the foreigners greeted each other. They spoke Russian fluently and with only the vaguest hint of an accent, as though they were used to Slavic pronunciations. Could they be from Poland? Czechoslovakia?

The man handed over a bag. Makarov opened it, peered inside, and passed it to Leonid. "Do your thing."

The geologist propped the bag on one of the stools, revealing the rough diamonds inside. They looked like chunks of glass. Still embedded in rock and dirt, they glinted in the pale light that emanated from the incandescent bulbs suspended along the ceiling.

Igor craned his neck and peered over Leonid's shoulder. "Whoa, those are some big rocks."

"They aren't cut. Cutting them will make them lose over half of their total volume," said Leonid.

He retrieved tools from his own bag: a jeweler's loupe, a microscope, and a few other items Igor didn't recognize.

Makarov relied on Leonid to authenticate precious stones and metals, which were the standard currency among the wealthy and the connected because the value of the ruble was in constant freefall.

Igor always thought his boss an eccentric for hiring a geologist. Any jeweler could have handled the task. Igor went to the library once, and read about identifying diamonds. He thought that even he could probably do a reasonable job of it, given a magnifying glass and a lighter. But, as was the case with his cars and his women, Makarov was accustomed to buying the best of everything, and that included hiring experts.

Leonid was taking his time, running all sorts of tests on the stones, and even studying some of the dirt they came with. Makarov opened one of the crates and was showing off a Kalashnikov to the two foreigners.

Igor studied the stones from a distance. In their rough form, they looked nothing like the gems he'd seen in the windows of expensive jewelry shops. It took a trained eye to recognize their true value, and a trained hand to cut the stone properly and bring all that potential to fruition. He couldn't help thinking how modern Russia was so much like a rough diamond: all that potential locked inside. But would it ever truly blossom into a gem if men like Makarov did the cutting?

Leonid carefully returned the stones to the bag, got up and waved Makarov over. While the foreigners were busy examining the merchandise, Makarov joined him. The two of them walked away and engaged in an animated discussion that lasted for nearly two minutes.

Makarov's men knew their boss; the expression on his face made them focus, primed them to expect trouble.

He confronted the foreigners. "What are you trying to pull?"

"Is there a problem?" asked the woman. She was holding a Kalashnikov, but Igor knew it wasn't loaded.

"You tell me." Makarov crossed his arms. "My expert tells me something is wrong about these stones."

"The precious stones were selected to your specifications," said the man.

Neither of the foreigners seemed nervous to Igor, but then, he supposed, arms merchants were accustomed to dangerous dealings.

"My geologist isn't happy," said Makarov. "And when he isn't happy, I get upset. Me being upset isn't good for business."

"Where are they from?" Leonid interjected himself into the conversation before Makarov could lose his cool and go too far with the threats. "There's no question these are authentic diamonds, but the impurities are highly unusual, and the lamproite matrix material is like nothing I've ever seen."

The two foreigners exchanged glances.

"You've already confirmed their authenticity," said the woman. "This should suffice. We prefer not to reveal the location of our mines."

"Not good enough," said Makarov. "If Leonid is suspicious, anyone I try to sell the diamonds to will be dubious as well."

"Meteoroid!" said Leonid. "They must've found extraterrestrial material with diamonds in it."

Everyone looked at the geologist.

"What, like from space?" asked Makarov.

"Earth has been bombarded by matter from space over the course of millions of years," said Leonid. "Some of it contains diamonds thought to be formed from the shock of collision between asteroids. All the ones I've heard of have been tiny, not like these." He puffed up, clearly proud of his deduction. "Most people wouldn't figure this out, but I was educated in Leningrad."

Makarov began to say something but was interrupted by the sound of gunfire outside.

Makarov's men reached for their weapons. It was what they were there for: extra muscle for a deal that presented an alluring target for anyone brazen enough to take advantage. No one outside of this warehouse was supposed to know when and where the exchange was going down. Igor didn't even know where he'd end up when Sharik picked him up earlier that evening. *Sharik!* He wasn't in the building. Could he have double-crossed them?

Makarov made eye contact with Igor and pointed at the foreigners. "Watch these two!" He turned to the others. "That crate over there. The guns in it are loaded."

Igor ushered his charges toward the far corner of the warehouse. He didn't think they were behind the attack. They'd arrived unarmed and had brought the gemstones. There was little for them to gain from the violence. Makarov must've made the same calculation, or his orders would have been different.

The deafening sound of an explosion nearly stunned Igor. It took him a few seconds to recover, and when he did he saw at least a dozen men with automatic rifles pouring in through the jagged hole blasted in the wall, advancing through the debris and the smoke.

The Chechens! Igor recognized a few of them from Makarov's past dealings. It couldn't have been Sharik, then. He hated the Chechens; if the dog was ever to betray his master, it wouldn't be to *them*.

The attackers advanced into the warehouse. Then they saw Makarov's men, armed with AK-47s. The two sides opened fire.

It was a bloodbath. Men on both sides died in a hail of bullets.

It must have been the adrenalin, but everything seemed to move very slowly to Igor. He thought the Chechens must have expected token resistance, must not have realized how many men Makarov would have or how well they would be armed, else they wouldn't walk into the enemy line of fire like this.

He held his pistol in both hands, reluctant to fire, reluctant to draw attention to himself and his unarmed wards. It worked for a short while. Then one of the Chechens turned his attention to him and the foreigners.

Igor and the attacker stared right at each other. Somehow, Igor was focusing on the wrong details: the bead of sweat on the man's forehead, the charcoal stain on his tan shirt. Igor couldn't bring himself to fire at a live target. The man turned his rifle toward him and squeezed the trigger.

A curtain of light, far brighter than the dim glow produced by the light bulbs, materialized between him and the attackers. Bullets bounced against the rectangular barrier as though it was a concrete wall. The impossible shield was pellucid and yet bright. Now everyone in the room was facing them.

Igor turned around to find one of the strangers focusing intently on a small sphere in his palm. The woman held a similar gadget, and cast wary glances at both groups of armed men.

It didn't take long for the Chechens to realize their bullets couldn't penetrate the barrier, and they went back to firing at Makarov and his men. The battle resumed, with Igor and the two foreigners stuck as spectators behind the light shield.

The entire skirmish couldn't have taken more than a minute, but it felt far longer to Igor. Powerless to act, but also thankful for the protection—however strange and incomprehensible the source of it was to him—he watched men die.

He saw Leonid fall backward, his body riddled with bullets. The light went out from the geologist's eyes.

This was what the guns Makarov was selling were meant to do, be it in Grozny, Chechnya or in some remote part of the world where they had palm trees. And now this violence was happening in front of him. Was happening *to* him.

He was too young to have personally experienced the horrors of the Soviet regime that he'd read about in the papers, but whatever atrocities the communists were guilty of, at least criminals hadn't battled it out openly in their time. He felt like he was seeing the end of civilization, the preview of things to come.

And who were these arms dealers exactly? Wizards? Time travelers? Aliens? He thought back to the extraterrestrial diamonds. Aliens fit the bill. He'd read Efremov, and Lem, and Bulychev. Aliens weren't supposed to be like this. Sinister or benevolent, what could they possibly want with a bunch of old AK-47 rifles? Although his mind was working in overdrive, it refused to process the surprise of the discovery, refused to cope with it. For now, whoever the foreigners were, they were keeping him safe and that was enough.

The fight ended with most of the Chechens dead or dying on the ground, and only a handful of the defenders, including Makarov himself, left standing. The last couple of intruders fled through the opening their explosive had created in the wall, Makarov's men firing at their backs.

The foreigner made the light shield disappear. Then they heard more shots from the outside, and more screams.

"Follow me," shouted Makarov as he raced toward Igor and the foreigners.

Whatever was coming next, he wanted the protection of the light shield, too. He and his men positioned themselves around the foreigners when yet another group entered the warehouse.

This time it was Sharik. He and his men advanced more carefully than the Chechens, entering the warehouse simultaneously through the front door and the blast hole in the wall.

Makarov held off ordering his men to fire, perhaps holding out hope that Sharik was still his loyal dog, that he had brought reinforcements to fight the Chechens. Igor thought his boss was a fool; Sharik was clearly making a power play and Makarov let his men come in and disperse along the walls. The foreigners were not so trusting. Both of them activated their light shields this time.

Sharik took a step forward and addressed Makarov's men.

"I'm in charge now." He pointed at Makarov. "There's room in my organization for whoever kills that pompous windbag."

A few of Makarov's men glanced at their boss, trying to figure out which way the wind was blowing.

"Are you kidding?" shouted Makarov. "You sicced the Chechens on us, tried to have us all killed. You think my men will trust you after that?"

"That wasn't personal," said Sharik. There was no remorse in his voice. "I let the two problems take care of each other; all my men have to do now is mop up. That's the kind of leadership those who join me can expect. You see, I take initiative." As he said that, he raised his pistol and shot at Makarov. The bullet made a whining sound as it ricocheted off the light barrier.

Sharik whistled. "I'll be damned." He cocked his head and stared at the foreigners with newfound interest. "You two, turn off your fancy American light-fence and I'll allow you to walk out of here."

The foreigners made no move to lower their shields.

"You have not proven yourself to be trustworthy," said the woman.

Sharik chuckled. "Suit yourselves." He waved to his men. "Take them."

Sharik's men had already dispersed throughout the warehouse. The defenders positioned themselves near the edges of the two light shields. The two groups sniped at one another, bullets whizzing across the warehouse.

Igor clutched his handgun in sweaty palms. A Hollywood action star would have taken charge, would have eliminated a half dozen opponents by himself. Igor thought he understood this sort of violence having seen it on badly dubbed videotapes, but real life was different. In real life he couldn't bring himself to engage. He huddled next to the foreigners and watched the events unfold around him.

Sharik ran along the far wall of the warehouse while his men laid cover fire. He got to the point where he had a clear shot, crouched and aimed.

The male arms dealer gasped and fell backward, a wet spot blossoming on his chest. The sphere rolled out of his hand and one of the light barriers flickered and went out. The woman screamed and dropped to her knees next to him, her barrier winking out of existence as well.

With their protection suddenly gone, the corner of the warehouse became a killing field. Sharik's men mowed down the defenders in a matter of seconds.

Igor crouched low, expecting a bullet to find him. He heard about people's lives flashing before their eyes in the final moments, but for him there was only terror and images of his family; how would they react when he didn't come home tonight? He imagined his parents arguing. Mom would want to file a missing persons report while Dad would say he was probably fine and they should wait until morning…

Makarov dove for the gadget dropped by the fallen foreigner. He grabbed hold of it but couldn't bring the defensive shield back to life. In his hands it was only a dead chunk of metal.

The woman cradled her partner's lifeless body and her wail turned into a scream of rage. She let go of his corpse, got up, grasped her own sphere with both hands and concentrated on it.

An intense wall of light formed several meters out, encircling the foreigners, Igor, Makarov and Tolya, one of his men. It blocked the bullets but left the rest of Makarov's people exposed to enemy fire.

The woman ignored the cacophony of gunfire and the screams of the wounded as she went on staring at the sphere. Suddenly the light burst outward like a sun going nova and bathed the entire warehouse. Then, less than a second later, it disappeared.

The warehouse was completely silent. Once Igor's eyes recovered from the flash of light, he could see that everyone on the outside of the barrier, Sharik's people and Makarov's alike, were dead. Their bodies were crumpled on the floor with no outward signs of any damage.

Makarov stared at the scene of the carnage for several long seconds, then turned to the woman who still held the sphere in both hands. Her wide eyes seemed unfocused, large tears pooling in their corners.

Makarov placed the sphere he'd been holding on the ground, took a step toward her and punched her in the face.

The woman crumpled onto the concrete. The sphere fell from her hands and Makarov kicked it out of reach. She clutched at her nose and blood poured through her fingers.

Igor noticed that the blood was orange. The same color as the bloodstain that covered the chest of her partner.

"What the devil are you?" asked Makarov.

The woman moaned softly, but made no response.

Makarov grabbed her by the shoulders and lifted her up. Then he forced her hands away from her face and studied her up close.

"You're some kind of a space alien, aren't you?" He shook her. "Answer me, or I'll put a bullet through your head."

"Yes," she whispered, her voice barely loud enough for Igor to hear. "We're from another world."

"Why are you here? What do you want with us?" Makarov asked.

"We told the truth. We want to trade for your weapons."

Makarov chuckled bitterly. "What do you want with guns, when you have… this." He nodded toward one of the spheres on the ground.

"We can't trade high technology on interdicted planets," she said. "Only mechanical weapons." She wiped the blood from her face with the sleeve of her jacket. "Our business model is like yours—outside the framework of our laws."

Makarov nodded, then called over his shoulder. "Guard her, Tolya. Igor, go find some rope and tie her up."

His remaining underling stepped up and trained his gun on the woman.

"We can still complete our transaction," she said. "You have the diamonds, and I can get you more."

"After all this, I'll need the guns *and* the diamonds," said Makarov. "Recruit new men, arm them. Besides, I have a feeling the CIA or some big corporation will pay me whatever I ask for you and your—what did you call it?—high technology. Enough to build an empire so strong no one will dare challenge me." He grinned savagely at Tolya. "Told you, stick with me and you'll make it big-time."

Igor thought it wasn't fair. The woman had saved their lives. He thought of the guns in the streets of his hometown, of the sort of violence a man like Makarov might unleash given the opportunity.

Makarov and Tolya were focused on the woman. They didn't see Igor raise his pistol. Even though his hands shook, it was impossible to miss at point-blank range. He put a bullet in the back of Makarov's head. Tolya began to turn, but he never had a chance: another pull of the trigger, and Igor and the woman remained the only ones alive in the building.

She trembled, no doubt expecting that the third bullet would be meant for her.

Igor stared at the carnage. "Tell me the truth, is it better…out there?" he asked, pointing upward with his gun.

She thought it over.

"No," she said, her voice small and resigned. "It is the same, everywhere."

Igor lowered his gun slowly.

"The weapons are yours," he said. "Get them out of here."

He understood that these guns would be used to kill, somewhere. He couldn't fix the whole universe. The only thing he could do, the only thing within his power, was to protect his tiny corner of it. Perhaps the heroes from Hollywood films would have found a better way, but Igor was no hero, and this wasn't a movie.

"Don't leave any behind, all right?"

Some of the tension slowly drained from the woman's face and she nodded.

Igor picked up the bag of diamonds, hefted it over his shoulder, and walked away without looking back.

Copyright © 2018 by Alex Shvartsman

TROPE-ING THE LIGHT
FANTASTIC
THE SCIENCE BEHIND THE FICTION

EDWARD M. LERNER

The essential resource for anyone who reads, writes, watches, or studies science fiction.

Men have walked on the Moon. Siri and Alexa manage—at least often enough to be helpful—to make sense of the things we say. Biologists have decoded DNA, and doctors have begun to tailor treatments to suit our individual genetic make-ups. In short: science and tech happen.

But faster-than-light travel? Time travel? Telepathy? A six million dollar—as adjusted, of course, for inflation—man? Starfaring aliens? Super-intelligent computers? Those, surely, are mere fodder for storytelling. Or wild extrapolations. Just so many "sci fi" tropes.

Sometimes, yes. But not necessarily.

In *Trope-ing the Light Fantastic*, physicist, computer engineer, science popularizer, and award-winning science-fiction author Edward M. Lerner entertainingly examines these and many other SF tropes. The science behind the fiction.

Each chapter, along with its eminently accessible scientific discussion, surveys science fiction—foundational and modern, in short and long written form, on TV and the big screen—that illustrates a particular trope. The good, the bad, and occasionally the cringe-worthy. All imparted with wit (and ample references to learn more).

So forget what the Wizard of Oz advised. Let's pull back the curtain…

APRIL 30, 2018   HARDCOVER   EBOOK

"A must-have for every science-fiction writer. Edward M. Lerner has produced the best-ever guide to putting the science in science fiction, and he's done it with clarity, wit, and panache. A terrific book — I'm recommending it to all my colleagues, and to all those who hope someday to be professional SF writers."
—**Robert J. Sawyer, Hugo Award-winning author of** *Quantum Night*

"This is a book which covers a huge number of topics well and provides great scientific and science fictional stimulation."
—**Dave Truesdale,** *Tangent Online*

"I am entertained and enlightened."
—**Larry Niven, author of** *Ringworld*

"A great source book for SF writers."
—**Bud Sparhawk, author of** *Distant Seas*

" …Worth your time, your money, and your consideration, whether you're interested in accessible science, looking to understand trends in science fiction, or—optimally—both."
—**Trevor Quachri, editor of** *Analog Science Fiction and Fact*
(excerpted from his guest foreword to the book)

Kristine Kathryn Rusch has won the Hugo as both a writer and an editor, and was recently nominated for a Shamus for Best Private Eye Novel. This is her eighth appearance in Galaxy's Edge.

THE FIRST STEP

by Kristine Kathryn Rusch

Harvey DeLeo's arthritic fingers shook as he reached for the small device. The clear case showed the blue workings, moving like liquid crystal. Most people would see shifting fractals.

He saw eternities.

"Dr. DeLeo, don't touch it." Annabelle Sharep, the fifteenth scientist to work on the project, the one whose insight made it all possible, stood on the other side of the lab.

She was a thin woman with a sharp chin. Because of that chin, he got her name wrong for the first year they worked together: he would call her Anna Sharp, and she would have to correct him.

Once she started chuckling and calling him the ultimate absent-minded professor, he learned her name. Or maybe he learned it because she was one of the few he had hired who could actually keep up with him mentally, someone who didn't harangue him, or tell him his hours were too long, or fret that he would damage his health.

The time for fretting had passed years ago.

And now, on its little protected pad, the device thrummed with life. In it, Annabelle saw futures.

With the device, they had sent pennies forward in time. They had sent cameras forward that recorded every image, except the images he wanted. The ones that had recorded the actual journey. It looked as if nothing had changed as the cameras traveled through time, as if the cameras had just stayed on the platform, and the scientists had been the ones who moved.

Finally, DeLeo and Annabelle had used actual living creatures to see if they would survive the journey. After the earthworms had survived, after the cockroaches had survived, after the rats had survived, DeLeo and Annabelle had taken the experiment to the next level, sending creatures two days into the future instead of five minutes.

DeLeo had been the one who decided to send creatures to the past to see what happened.

Those were the experiments that showed time travel operated differently going backward in time than it did going forward. If an object already existed in the past, the object being sent back would become a ghostly reflection of itself.

Those had been the only experiments that freaked out the rats—DeLeo and Annabelle soon realized that cockroaches and earthworms weren't self aware enough to get freaked out. Or perhaps DeLeo and Annabelle didn't know what a freaked-out cockroach looked like.

Those experiments also led to the occasional death, particularly among the rats. DeLeo wasn't a biologist, so he didn't know if the freaked-out rats had ended up with scrambled thoughts or if that ghostly separation had caused an actual physical reaction.

Annabelle had started a partnership with some colleagues in biology to see what was happening on a molecular level.

DeLeo didn't really care. One trip to the past would be worth an early death, at least for him.

DeLeo's fingers hovered over the device. He had to activate it, and simultaneously put his hand flat on white disk Annabelle laughingly called "the launch pad." He wasn't sure the launch pad was big enough to handle him. He wasn't sure what would happen to his body when he did this. He wasn't sure if he would destroy the whole project with this attempt.

But none of that would stop him.

"Dr. DeLeo, don't touch. It's too soon," Annabelle said. "We've had this discussion."

They had too.

At every point along the way, they had had some version of this discussion.

Inventors shouldn't be the first to use their inventions, Annabelle had said one afternoon.

Alexander Graham Bell did, DeLeo had replied.

He invented the telephone, Annabelle had said. *It couldn't hurt him.*

We know that now, DeLeo had said. *They didn't know it then.*

It's not the same, Annabelle had said, *and you know it.*

Maybe DeLeo did know it. Maybe he didn't. He had theories about what happened to the creatures that went to the past and appeared with a ghostly sort of shape. He believed that shape was a manifestation of their consciousness—and yes, he believed all living things had a consciousness.

Annabelle didn't. She thought that matter somehow arrived in the past, then discovered it was already there—and that was where DeLeo tuned her out every single time.

As a young scientist, he would have listened. He would have argued, if need be. He would have *learned*.

But he wasn't doing this for the learning. Or the glory. Or even for a second success.

He was doing it for one moment.

He activated the sequence he had already programmed into the device and placed his palm on the launch pad. Annabelle was screaming at him. Other lab assistants were running through the open door.

They became insubstantial, and then they whisked away. The room became what it had been forty-five years before, a gigantic old classroom filled with wooden desks, initials and graffiti carved into the seatbacks. To his right, the old closet that he would later transform into his new office.

There was no device here, no launch pad, and probably no elderly Doctor DeLeo, although he seemed substantial enough to himself.

He was standing alone inside that classroom and he thought he smelled chalk. He probably didn't. It was most likely a sense memory, but he didn't care.

He knew he had to move quickly.

The classroom's door stood open, like all of the rooms did at this time of day—just after eleven p.m. as the janitor made his rounds. Amazing the trivia a man still remembered after forty-five years of living. A human brain slowly filled up with useless junk.

Who knew that an ancient, irrelevant detail would become so important now.

DeLeo walked through an aisle between desks, then out the door into the wide corridor. The floor was the gray and black 1950s tile that had first suggested the device to him—back when his office was three doors down. He walked past that office and couldn't resist a glance.

There he was, his thirty-year-old self, hovering over some components that the elderly DeLeo didn't even recognize.

A familiar sadness squeezed his heart. He paused, thought about all the time paradoxes—if he said something, if he gave a hint about the future, if he even gave his old self a heads-up about the present—what would change?

DeLeo didn't want to risk changing anything.

This day, the next hour, were the reasons he had built the device. Not so that graduate students in religion could travel back to Christ's crucifixion to see if it really happened as the Bible said. Not so that historians could add to their dissertations by actually speaking to Thomas Jefferson. Not so that techs could fruitlessly try to modify the device so that someone could finally shoot Hitler.

DeLeo had built the device for this, this short future—or this short past—or this short whatever someone wanted to call the next few minutes; *this* was the reason the device existed. He had a hunch no one would ever know what he had done, what his motivations were, why he had used the device before it got tested all the way up the biological food chain, hell, before all the computer modeling was even finished.

He had a hunch he would die before he could tell them.

He was seventy-five years old with a defective heart, and a possible death sentence, and if he waited for everything to be perfect, he would make the same mistake twice.

DeLeo went down the stairs like he used to as a young man, almost running as he bounced his way down. The old corridors, the old wooden doors, the old janitor (who was probably younger than DeLeo was now) pushing a bucket into the men's room—how many nights had DeLeo seen this very scenario and never really noticed it?

His one worry—the exterior door—stood open, sending in chill January air. It smelled of snow, although he wondered if that too was his imagination.

He crossed the quad to the graduate student housing, half expecting the students he passed to yell, "Hey, Prof, what're you doing outside the lab?" like they did these days or in the future or whenever now really was.

But the wind was strong, and everyone had their heads bowed against it, hoods pulled up over their faces. They weren't looking at him.

The campus had dimmer lighting, less of it too, before the anti-violence advocates finally convinced the administration that a well-lit campus was a safer campus. (It turned out to be true.)

Still, even in the semi-darkness, he could find his way to that little house, attached on each side to other little houses with their paper-thin walls and overactive heating systems. That pre—World War II housing got torn down twenty years ago or would get torn down twenty-five years from now, and (would be) replaced with a big new athletic center. Whenever he saw the glistening thing, his heart squeezed sadly, painfully.

He preferred these drab little buildings with their yellow incandescent lights spilling out into the postage-stamp yards. Those little buildings had hope, and possibility.

The real kind, not the athletic kind.

He walked up his old front porch, knowing the doors wouldn't be open. Margery had always kept the doors closed and locked when DeLeo wasn't home, which meant the doors had always been closed and locked.

But the windows were open, because that little house was always fifteen degrees too warm.

He settled near the picture window, and waited.

Margery walked into the room, wearing a pair of sweatpants and one of his old T-shirts from Cal-Tech. She looked tired and oh, so beautiful, still a bit of baby weight on her hips.

Then he heard it, that familiar little voice, one he had forgotten after it had gotten replaced decades ago with a deep baritone: "Maaaa?"

She laughed and turned, looking in the direction of the coffee table.

DeLeo couldn't see anything. His eyes filled with hopeless old man tears. All of this, and he couldn't see anything.

He stood on his tiptoes, and finally, the baby came into view. Not a baby any more. That nanosecond between infant and full toddler, right on the brink. His son Richard, named for DeLeo's father, the warm man who had done his grandfather duties right, thank heavens, because Richard had needed a male role model, and DeLeo hadn't been it.

"Maaaaa," Richard said, chubby hands reaching, grasping, clutching.

DeLeo wiped at his eyes furiously. He had to see this without tears. He had to see…

Richard's fingers caught the edge of the table, and pulled. DeLeo's breath caught. His son rose just an inch, then tumbled backward.

Margery started to go to him, but stopped as Richard—determined even then—sat back up. He adjusted his diaper-clad bottom, got on his dimpled knees, and placed his hands firmly on that table. Then he lifted himself up, one shaky limb at a time.

Margery put her fingers over her mouth. Richard gave her a toothless baby grin.

DeLeo frowned. He hadn't come for standing. He had watched Richard stand once before way back then, although to be honest, DeLeo hadn't paid much attention.

Yeah, yeah, he'd been thinking at the time. *A baby standing. So what?*

So what. He got to see his pretty wife again, that's what. And his pure perfect infant son.

DeLeo swallowed hard now, stared. Margery didn't move. For a moment, DeLeo thought she could see him, but she was still looking at their son. At *her* son. DeLeo had just contributed DNA, really. Never home, never there, never thinking about them. All charges—accurate charges—in the divorce. If only he had been home. If only he had cared—even a little—for the small things.

If only he understood that precious events happened only once.

Richard waved a hand, looking sideways. He clearly saw the old man at the window, probably thought that was his Grandpop, and gave DeLeo a big toothless grin. DeLeo smiled back, hoped his loitering there wouldn't change the moment.

Then Richard turned toward his mother, used the flat surface to keep himself upright and leaned-walked toward her. He reached the edge of the table and kept going, walking, stumbling really, moving with determined little steps, and falling into her arms.

Six seconds, maybe less, seconds she had brought (would bring?) up in an argument two days later.

Until that fight, DeLeo hadn't even known his child —the boy that would be his *only* child—had taken his first steps.

First steps missed, like the first word, and the first day of school, as well as the last day of school and the first graduation ceremony. The first date, the first prom. DeLeo made it for the first (only) marriage, but not the birth of the first grandchild or the second or the third, and all of those first steps, first words, first loves. He was not the grandfather his own father had been, and DeLeo wouldn't have known how to try, even though, by then, he wanted to.

All those missed events—only seconds long, really—all that missed time.

He wasn't making up for it here. He had hoped (deep down) there might be alternate timelines, ways of influencing, maybe even becoming, someone else, but there weren't. Just the ghostly consciousness, and the observation.

And, as the experimentation had revealed that, DeLeo had realized he would only get one vision, one visit, one missed event, and he had thought and thought and thought about which one to choose.

He had finally decided on this one, the one that still made his heart squeeze when he heard the phrase "baby's first…", the first missed event he really and truly regretted.

Not that it changed anything. For anyone except him.

Voices sounded around him, and he saw a ghostly lab slowly superimposing itself over his old home. He would return to the lab in a heartbeat.

He made himself focus that living room, instead of the encroaching lab, on his wife, her arms around their son, praising him for his toddling steps, and the boy, squirming to get away and do it again, so very Richard, even back then.

His wife reached for her phone to record this moment—the second attempt at walking. She would prove successful, and the time stamp that DeLeo had stared at over and over again had proven to be accurate.

DeLeo had worried that this moment, these six seconds, wouldn't live up to his expectations. He had worried that an old miracle, one so obvious, one completed by most human babies, completed by Richard's babies and to be completed by their babies, would seem anti-climactic.

But it wasn't.

DeLeo used to think he had lost eternities of precious time, but he hadn't.

He had worked an eternity to gain an eternity.

In six seconds.

And at the end of them, just before the lab became the only reality, DeLeo's baby boy—the baby his boy had been—the *happy* baby his boy had been—raised his tiny fists in triumph and joy.

Like DeLeo used to do whenever he succeeded.

No one had told him Richard had done that.

Maybe no one had noticed.

But DeLeo did.

At the last second of his eternity. Making each and every moment of his entire lifetime worthwhile.

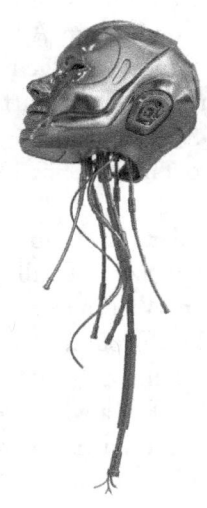

This marks Laurence Raphael Brother's first appearance in Galaxy's Edge. *His previous work has appeared in* New Haven Review, Nature *magazine,* PodCastle *publications, and elsewhere.*

THE VIOLET HOUR

by Laurence Raphael Brothers

We were all eager to meet the special stagecoach carrying the new marshal, but in the end we held back. We figured he might lose his composure if a whole bunch of us was crowding around him right from the start. He'd traveled miles and miles into the Earth, from the light of the surface into the murk of the underworld. It used to be a narrow, dangerous path that no one in their right mind would ever take, but our miners had cleared it to the point that a coach could go the whole way. Anyhow, none of us locals was there to meet the stage except for the hostler Jonesy, who was human and from the States.

Course, I expected the marshal to visit me first thing. But it was a right surprise when the door to my office swung open and in walked a woman. Shouldn't have been shocked, being female myself, but still. She wore a businesslike blue dress with a Colt Peacemaker on her hip. A badge was pinned to her chest. Not a deputy's badge neither: full marshal. I had a star on my vest too, dwarf-mined gold, but it wasn't as official.

She paused to take me in. Didn't boggle at all, which I liked.

"Mrs. F.M. Miller," she said. "US Marshal, New Territories. Or that's what I will be when the papers get signed back in Washington. A pleasure."

"Kallitoxotis, sheriff 'round here. Likewise, I'm sure."

"You speak excellent English."

"Thanks," I said. "For a while now, best way to get here's been from the entrance in Nevada, the Carson range, I think you call it?" She nodded and I continued. "Before your people showed up we got the occasional medicine man on a quest, but now sometimes we get prospectors, explorers, folks like that. Not many, but enough to tell us how things are going. So we can keep up to date on life topside, second-hand like."

She held out her hand. A strong, firm grip.

"Please sit down," I said. "You'll excuse me for not doing the same."

"Of course." She drew a chair up before my standing desk. "Listen, Sheriff, I know this is hasty, but I wonder if you have time to discuss jurisdiction? I expect this will go better if we can set some boundaries up front, so we all know what's what."

"Sure thing, ma'am," I said. "Always good to know where we stand."

We were discussing whose law was going to govern whose people during the transition period when my deputy Teoxihuitl busted in. The marshal gave him more of an eye than she had me, but then he was dressed mainly in turquoise, and not much turquoise neither.

"Sheriff!" he said, panting. "It's those Utgard boys. They're tearing up the saloon!"

"Damnation! Marshal, scuse us, would you? This one's mine to deal with."

"Yes," she said. "Yours for sure. But I'd like to come along, if I may."

"Your funeral," I said, regretting it right away. Never tempt the Moirai.

I paused to grab my bow and sling a quiver, stringing the old recurve by bracing it against my right front hoof. The bartender Eugenios was the only one in town I could talk with about old times back in Aeolia. My last link to the past. I wanted to race to the saloon to make sure he was okay. But no way Teo and the marshal could keep up.

She looked up at me as I pranced in indecision. "May I ride with you?"

"You follow us up," I told Teo. I hoisted the marshal up with one arm, and settled her on my back before galloping the mile to the saloon. She was a good horsewoman; and so was I, but not the same way. We passed through a mile of darkened mushroom caves, shy Nimerigar farmers staying hidden though they knew full well who I was. And then we emerged from the tunnel and entered the great world-cavern, the vast inner space that underlay the bright lands of the surface.

It was the violet hour in the katakosmos—whoops, the New Territories now. But the corelight from the inner sun illuminating the Hollow Earth was never very bright. That was one reason

I was in favor of admission to the States. It'd been a long time since I'd seen the sun, the real one I mean, and a long time since I felt a proper wind in my mane, or heard the cries of birds overhead. We'd always had a trickle of human visitors, finding their way down here from the surface from entrances like the Acheron or the Cumaean Gate, but we'd never reached out to them before. But lately we'd been learning about the United States, how they'd gotten rid of slavery, and about their constitutional amendments that guaranteed freedom to all. Seemed to us like this was something new in the world. Seemed like we might have rights if we joined up, like we might not have to worry about massacres and running away to hide in our underworld anymore. So we all got together and we all said our pieces, and when we voted it was pretty much all in favor.

I was anxious about Eugenios, so I might have been galloping harder than I should given I had a rider to worry about, but Mrs. Miller had a good seat, and I didn't hardly have to slow down at all for her. Soon we got to the town proper, with the general store, the outfitter, the barber, the big smithy, and the saloon. There was a small crowd of kobold and lutin miners milling around outside. A gray-skinned kobold foreman came up to me as I was handing the marshal down.

"Sorry, Sheriff," he said. "Somehow those damn jotnar got their hands on some liquor back at the mine. We couldn't stop them after that. You know how they get. Eugenios is inside with them."

"Anyone killed or hurt bad?"

He shook his head. "Not yet."

"Jotnar?" asked the marshal. She looked excited.

"Giants," I said. "Mean drunks, too. Positive you want to come in with me?"

"Yup." I liked her pluck.

I ducked inside through the shattered saloon doors, the marshal right behind me. Sure enough, the three jotunn brothers were there. Gangr was passed out in a corner, his huge bulk sodden in the remains of a ruptured ale barrel. Idi was sitting splaylegged on the floor guzzling whiskey; he looked up, saw me, choked and fell back insensible. Thjazi was at the bar, hunched over to keep his head from bumping the rafters, and—*shit*—he had his

huge pickaxe up against Eugenios' throat. A trickle of blood was already running down the faun's neck. The bartender looked imploringly at me but he couldn't say anything.

"Thjazi," I said, "let him go or by the gods—" My bow was at full draw, a broad-headed arrow targeting the giant's heart.

"By the gods?" Thjazi turned to face me. "What gods're those, Sheriff? Utgardaloki is gone. Surtr's gone too. My little girl Skadi…dead like the Aesir, dead as your 'lympians. No one knows our names or our deeds, and we got no more kin in this whole wide underworld. Even Yggdrasil's roots don't reach this far down. So you may's well let fly, horsey girl. We just don't give a damn anymore."

I was thinking maybe I *should* just put Thjazi out of his misery, but I wasn't sure a single arrow would do for him, and I'd never forgive myself if Eugenios got hurt. So I hesitated, and while I dithered, the marshal stepped forward, surprising me. The giant glanced at her and leered, but she spoke up before he could say anything.

"Thjazi. Thjazi of Utgard. Your brothers are Gangr and Idi. Strong sons of Alvadi, mouths gaping with gold."

Huh. The marshal sounded different now. Like she was speaking another language.

Thjazi's eyes widened. "Who're you to know our kennings?" He lowered his pickaxe, and Eugenios slumped away without the giant noticing. I could have shot him then, but the marshal put her hand on my withers so I held back.

"I'm the new marshal hereabouts. Mrs. Miller."

"Why should I care—"

"Because I tell you to." The marshal had an aura about her now. I remembered seeing something like that, long ago. Back in the old days, when shining Apollo would stop by our halls to visit his godson Chiron. Was that a six-gun at the marshal's waist, or was she holding a bright-bladed spear? And her sensible dress…now a gleaming byrnie of polished mail? I blinked, seeing double.

"Don't you even know me, Thjazi?"

"Uh…." The giant was slack-jawed.

"I was a widow many times over before I married my dear Mr. Miller. My first husband was Odr."

"Odr? *Odr?* Th-then you must be—"

"Freyja Marigold Miller. US Marshal. And you boys are a disgrace."

"Oh! Freyja!" Thjazi started to cry.

"There," said the marshal. She stepped closer, raised her hand to stroke his grizzled cheek. "There. Don't cry. What would Alvadi think if he could see you sniffling like that?"

Thjazi blinked, wiped his nose. "Shouldn't—ain't we s'posed to be enemies?"

"That's over," said the marshal. "Over and done. There's a new dispensation in Midgard, too. They passed something called the fifteenth amendment. What it means—"

Thjazi dropped his pickaxe. He was snoring, his head cradled in the marshal's arms. She laid the giant's bulk out on the floor, effortlessly despite his enormous size.

"Well," she said. "That's done with. Happy to be of service." She held out her hand to me, but I was goggling at her, too much in awe to take it.

Eugenios knelt before Mrs. Miller, his horned head bowed. I think he was crying too.

I was nearly tongue-tied. "Should I, uh, honor you or something, ma'am? You're one of the gods?"

"Once upon a time, maybe," said the marshal. "Thjazi was right though; the age of the gods is over. Now I'm just a law-woman. Same as you."

"Same as me?"

"Near as makes no difference. Not anymore."

She gave me her hand again, and I took it.

Stories by Karlo Yeager Rodriguez have appeared in Nature, Clowns, *and* Pulp Literature. *This is his first appearance in* Galaxy's Edge.

EMERGENCY EVALUATION FOR PENNY ANTE, AS RECORDED BY CAL-Q-TRON OF THE BENEVOLENT ORDER OF HEROES

by Karlo Yeager Rodríguez

Summary: Penelope G. Macías (a.k.a., "Penny Ante," henceforth referred to as "Penny") was selected last year to be a sidekick to Major Patriot (henceforth "the Major"—at his own insistence). After some initial friction over the sidekick handle selected for her by the Major, Penny settled into her new role. She was on track to accomplish Supers certification within record time. Penny's recent behavior forced this unit to perform a re-evaluation at the Major's request. Penny's time requirement for Supers eligibility and certification will be extended as per Section 14.1 (i) of the Benevolent Order of Heroes, Twin Cities (Minneapolis) Chapter bylaws.

Job Knowledge: 5.0 (Outstanding) Penny learns and applies new skills much quicker than most of her colleagues. She anticipates and conducts further research in a self-directed way.

Strengths: Penny thwarted an attack by the St. Paul Sinister Sisters. She defused Herr Doktor's Bald-O-Matic Ray before the Major arrived on the scene.

Opportunities: She was instrumental in protecting the world from premature hair loss. However, her failure to adhere to proper chain-of-command protocols ("Robin's Rulebook," pages 14, 78-82) ensured the Major appeared befuddled and uninformed before TV news drones. Penny *did* text the Major, but since he was in stasis from 1937 to last year, he has yet to adjust to this new technology.

Productivity: 2.5 (Meets Expectations) Penny completes the requisite amount of work within the timeframe needed. However, she resists taking on extra tasks, as per section 3.3 of the Order's bylaws

("Teamwork and Leadership") and "Robin's Rulebook," (pages 2-10). One such example is her refusal to sort the Major's treasured marble collection by size, color and type (clearies, steelies and so on) regardless of his many requests.

Opportunities: Penny exploited a flaw in Automatron's look-alike bots, making them go haywire. The Sinister Sisters' cyborg member was stunned, but easy to ID and apprehend by other members of the Order. However, Penny neglected to help the team contain the damage caused by the out-of-control robot minions. A more productive use of Penny's time would have been to ask where she could help instead of linking robot bodies to spell out "WREKT."

Initiative: 4.0 (Exceeds Expectations) Penny is motivated, starting and finishing tasks with minimal supervision.

Strengths: On her own, Penny designed and created the SupersAlert! app. The public can now log suspected villain activity from their phones rather than using lighted signals or other similar beacons, which only work on overcast nights.

Opportunities: Penny's initiative has not translated into her taking more of a lead role in the Order.

Communication: 1.5 (Needs Improvement) As referenced, Penny's inefficient communication with her team has led to several incidents. This core competency affects her performance in many other areas.

Strengths: Penny improved communication between the general public and the Order through her app. This has helped her team defend the Twin Cities from the Sinister Sisters.

Opportunities: Recent situations where Penny could have communicated better follow.

- Communication includes tailoring messages to fit the intended recipient. Limit text alerts to the Major until after he completes all forthcoming training modules on modern telecommunication technology.

- Professionalism is of utmost importance. Your behavior impacts how the Order appears to outside observers, and can embolden enemies.
  For example:
  o Hijacking the Harbinger's cosmic surfboard and taking it for a joyride during diplomatic negotiations led to a galactic incident between the Order and interstellar Shree Empire.
  o The height of the Shree's interstellar invasion is not the time to post a selfie on social media.

- Delegating work to fellow sidekicks—such as picking up the Major's dry cleaning—is not an acceptable practice, no matter how heavy a workload the Major gave you (see "Robin's Rulebook," pages 7-8, 36, 48 and 325-330).

Summary: Penny is a valued addition to the team who displays her genius at analysis, but has not yet achieved the full promise of her abilities. Given the mentioned infractions of the Order's bylaws, and the Major's input, we have reached a decision. The Benevolent Order of Heroes, Twin Cities (Minneapolis) Chapter, agrees to postpone Penny's promotion to full-fledged Super until she completes the "Next Steps" (see below).

Next Steps: Due to Penny's issues with communication, we stress more open communications with peers and higher-ups. This unit suggests she focus on learning the Major's preferences, since his recommendation is important to her promotion. This unit will assign Penny both the "Interpersonal Relations" and "The Seven Languages of Effective Supers" trainings before resuming everyday duties. This unit will also extend the probationary sidekick period for another two years. This should ensure Penny's Supers certification will occur when she's better prepared to take on the added responsibility. During this time, we invite her to review her copy of "Robin's Rulebook" often, ask the Major questions any time she has doubts, and not forget this unit's "Open Input/Output Ports" policy regarding any concerns she may have.

Acknowledgement: I have reviewed this document and discussed the content with a chosen representative of the Benevolent Order of Heroes, Twin Cities (Minneapolis) Chapter. By signing this document, I agree that I have been advised of my performance status only, with no implication I agree with the evaluation.

Employee Signature _____

Date: _____

Benevolent Order of Heroes Rep: CAL Q TRON, iPhD

Notes: Penny refused to sign, even when encouraged to do so under protest. She uttered precisely seventeen florid descriptions of my parentage as well as the Major's (impossible, since I am a machine—I cannot speak for the Major). She surrendered her Order-issued gear (see attached inventory) and asked if the Major's incompetence fell under "Job Knowledge." Twelve datapoints in how she said this make me estimate it was sarcasm.

Her wondering aloud "if the Sinister Sisters were recruiting," however, was not.

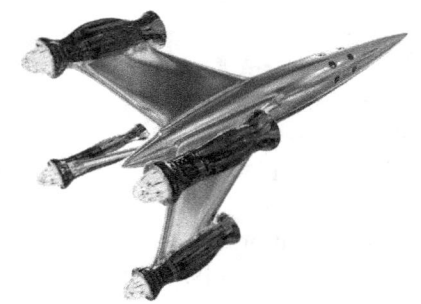

Gardner Dozois is known primarily as an editor, winning an amazing fourteen Best Editor Hugos during his time at Asimov's. *But Gardner is a writer too, and indeed won two Nebula Awards for short stories before winning any of his editing awards.*

A DREAM AT NOONDAY

by Gardner Dozois

I remember the sky, and the sun burning in the sky like a golden penny flicked into a deep blue pool, and the scuttling white clouds that changed into magic ships and whales and turreted castles as they drifted up across that bottomless ocean and swam the equally bottomless sea of my mind's eye. I remember the winds that skimmed the clouds, smoothing and rippling them into serene grandeur or boiling them into froth. I remember the same wind dipping low to caress the grass, making it sway and tremble, or whipping through the branches of the trees and making them sing with a wild, keening organ note. I remember the silence that was like a bronzen shout echoing among the hills.

—It is raining. The sky is slate-gray and grittily churning. It looks like a soggy dishrag being squeezed dry, and the moisture is dirty rain that falls in pounding sheets, pressing down the tall grass. The rain pocks the ground, and the loosely packed soil is slowly turning into mud, and the rain spatters the mud, making it shimmer—

And I remember the trains. I remember lying in bed as a child, swathed in warm blankets, sniffing suspiciously and eagerly at the embryonic darkness of my room, and listening to the big trains wail and murmur in the freight yard beyond. I remember lying awake night after night, frightened and darkly fascinated, keeping very still so that the darkness wouldn't see me, and listening to the hollow booms and metallic moans as the trains coupled and linked below my window. I remember that I thought the trains were alive, big dark beasts who came to dance and to hunt each other through the dappled moonlight of the world outside my room, and when I would listen to the whispering clatter of their passing and feel the room quiver ever so slightly in shy response, I would get a crawly feeling in my chest and a prickling along the back of my neck, and I would wish that I could watch them dance, although I knew that I never would. And I remember that it was different when I watched the trains during the daytime, for then even though I clung tight to my mother's hand and stared wide-eyed at their steam-belching and spark-spitting they were just big iron beasts putting on a show for me; they weren't magic then, they were hiding the magic inside them and pretending to be iron beasts and waiting for the darkness. I remember that I knew even then that trains are only magic in the night and only dance when no one can see them. And I remember that I couldn't go to sleep at night until I was soothed by the muttering lullaby of steel and the soft, rhythmical hiss-clatter of a train booming over a switch. And I remember that some nights the bellowing of a fast freight or the cruel, whistling shriek of a train's whistle would make me tremble and feel cold suddenly, even under my safe blanket-mountain, and I would find myself thinking about rain-soaked ground and blood and black cloth and half-understood references to my grandfather going away, and the darkness would suddenly seem to curl in upon itself and become diamond-hard and press down upon my straining eyes, and I would whimper and the fading whistle would snatch the sound from my mouth and trail it away into the night. And I remember that at times like that I would pretend that I had tiptoed to the window to watch the trains dance, which I never really dared to do because I knew I would die if I did, and then I would close my eyes and pretend that I was a train, and in my mind's eye I would be hanging disembodied in the darkness a few inches above the shining tracks, and then the track would begin to slip along under me, slowly at first then fast and smooth like flowing syrup, and then the darkness would be flashing by and then I would be moving out and away, surrounded by the wailing roar and evil steel chuckling of a fast freight slashing through the night, hearing my whistle scream with the majestic cruelty of a stooping eagle and feeling the switches boom and clatter hollowly

under me, and I would fall asleep still moving out and away, away and out.

—The rain is stopping slowly, trailing away across the field, brushing the ground like long, dangling gray fingers. The wet grass creeps erect again, bobbing drunkenly, shedding its burden of water as a dog shakes himself dry after a swim. There are vicious little crosswinds in the wake of the storm, and they make the grass whip even more violently than the departing caress of the rain. The sky is splitting open above, black rain clouds pivoting sharply on a central point, allowing a sudden wide wedge of blue to appear. The overcast churns and tumbles and clots like wet heavy earth turned by a spade. The sky is now a crazy mosaic of mingled blue and gray. The wind picks up, chews at the edge of the tumbling wrack, spinning it to the fineness of cotton candy and then lashing it away. A broad shaft of sunlight falls from the dark undersides of the clouds, thrusting at the ground and drenching it in a golden cathedral glow, filled with shimmering green highlights. The effect is like that of light through a stained-glass window, and objects bathed in the light seem to glow very faintly from within, seem to be suddenly translated into dappled molten bronze. There is a gnarled, shaggy tree in the center of the pool of sunlight, and it is filled with wet, disgruntled birds, and the birds are hesitantly, cautiously, beginning to sing again—

And I remember wandering around in the woods as a boy and looking for nothing and finding everything and that clump of woods was magic and those rocks were a rustlers' fort and there were dinosaurs crashing through the brush just out of sight and everybody knew that there were dragons swimming in the sea just below the waves and an old glittery piece of Coke bottle was a magic jewel that could let you fly or make you invisible and everybody knew that you whistled twice and crossed your fingers when you walked by that deserted old house or something shuddery and scaly would get you and you argued about bang you're dead no I'm not and you had a keen gun that could endlessly dispatch all the icky monsters who hung out near the swing set in your backyard without ever running out of ammunition. And I remember that as a kid I was nuts about finding a magic cave and I used to think that there was a cave under every rock, and I would get a long stick to use as a lever and I would sweat and strain until I had managed to turn the rock over, and then when I didn't find any tunnel under the rock I would think that the tunnel was there but it was just filled in with dirt, and I would get a shovel and I would dig three or four feet down looking for the tunnel and the magic cave and then I would give up and go home for a dinner of beans and franks and brown bread. And I remember that once I did find a little cave hidden under a big rock and I couldn't believe it and I was scared and shocked and angry and I didn't want it to be there but it was and so I stuck my head inside it to look around because something wouldn't let me leave until I did and it was dark in there and hot and very still and the darkness seemed to be blinking at me and I thought I heard something rustling and moving and I got scared and I started to cry and I ran away and then I got a big stick and came back, still crying, and pushed and heaved at that rock untill it thudded back over the cave and hid it forever. And I remember that the next day I went out again to hunt for a magic cave.

—The rain has stopped. A bird flaps wetly away from the tree and then settles back down onto an outside branch. The branch dips and sways with the bird's weight, its leaves heavy with rain. The tree steams in the sun, and a million raindrops become tiny jewels, microscopic prisms, gleaming and winking, loving and transfiguring the light even as it destroys them and they dissolve into invisible vapor puffs to be swirled into the air and absorbed by the waiting clouds above. The air is wet and clean and fresh; it seems to squeak as the wet grass saws through it and the wind runs its fingernails lightly along its surface. The day is squally and gusty after the storm, high shining overcast split by jagged ribbons of blue that look like aerial fjords, The bird preens and fluffs its feathers disgustedly, chattering and scolding at the rain, but keeping a tiny bright eye carefully, cocked in case the storm should take offense at the liquid stream of insults and come roaring back. Between the tufts of grass the ground has turned to black mud, soggy as a sponge, puddled by tiny pools of steaming rainwater. There is an arm and a hand lying in the mud, close enough to make out the texture of the tattered fabric clothing the arm, so close that the upper arm fades up and past the viewpoint and into a huge featureless blur in the extreme corner of the field of vision. The arm is bent back at an unnatural angle and the stiff fingers are hooked into talons that seem to claw toward the gray sky—

And I remember a day in the sixth grade when we were struggling in the cloakroom with our coats and snow-encrusted overshoes and I couldn't get mine off because one of the snaps had frozen shut and Denny was talking about how his father was a jet pilot and he sure hoped the war wasn't over before he grew up because he wanted to kill some Gooks like his daddy was doing and then later in the boy's room everybody was arguing about who had the biggest one and showing them and Denny could piss farther than anybody else. I remember that noon at recess we were playing kick the can and the can rolled down the side of the hill and we all went down after it and somebody said hey look and we found a place inside a bunch of bushes where the grass was all flattened down and broken and there were pages of a magazine scattered all over and Denny picked one up and spread it out and it was a picture of a girl with only a pair of pants on and everybody got real quiet and I could hear the girls chanting in the schoolyard as they jumped rope and kids yelling and everybody was scared and her eyes seemed to be looking back right out of the picture and somebody finally licked his lips and said what're those things stickin' out of her, ah, and he didn't know the word and one of the bigger kids said tits and he said yeah what're those things stickin' outta her tits and I couldn't say anything because I was so surprised to find out that girls had those little brown things like we did except that hers were pointy and hard and made me tremble and Denny said hell I knew about that I've had hundreds of girls but he was licking nervously at his lips as he said it and he was breathing funny too. And I remember that afternoon I was sitting at my desk near the window and the sun was hot and I was being bathed in the rolling drone of our math class and I wasn't understanding any of it and listening to less. I remember that I knew I had to go to the bathroom but I didn't want to raise my hand because our math teacher was a girl with brown hair and eyeglasses and I was staring at the place where I knew her pointy brown things must be under her blouse and I was thinking about touching them to see what they felt like and that made me feel funny somehow and I thought that if I raised my hand she would be able to see into my head and she'd know and she'd tell everybody what I was thinking and then she'd get mad and punish me for thinking bad things and so I didn't say anything but I had to go real bad and if I looked real close I thought that I could see two extra little bulges in her blouse where her pointy things were pushing against the cloth and I started thinking about what it would feel like if she pushed them up against me and that made me feel even more funny and sort of hollow and sick inside and I couldn't wait any longer and I raised my hand and left the room but it was too late and I wet myself when I was still on the way to the boys' room and I didn't know what to do so I went back to the classroom with my pants all wet and smelly and the math teacher looked at me and said what did you do and I was scared and Denny yelled he pissed in his pants he pissed in his pants and I said I did not the water bubbler squirted me but Danny yelled he pissed in his pants he pissed in his pants and the math teacher got very mad and everybody was laughing and suddenly the kids in my class didn't have any faces but only laughing mouths and I wanted to curl up into a ball where nobody could get me and once I had seen my mother digging with a garden spade and turning over the wet dark earth and there was half of a worm mixed in with the dirt and it writhed and squirmed until the next shovelful covered it up.

—Most of the rain has boiled away, leaving only a few of the larger puddles that have gathered in the shallow depressions between grass clumps. The mud is slowly solidifying under the hot sun, hardening into ruts, miniature ridges and mountains and valleys. An ant appears at the edge of the field of vision, emerging warily from the roots of the wet grass, pushing its way free of the tangled jungle. The tall blades of grass tower over it, forming a tightly interwoven web and filtering the hot yellow sunlight into a dusky green half-light. The ant pauses at the edge of the muddy open space, reluctant to exchange the cool tunnel of the grass for the dangers of level ground. Slowly, the ant picks its way across the sticky mud, skirting a pebble half again as big as it is. The pebble is streaked with veins of darker rock and has a tiny flake of quartz embedded in it near the top. The elements have rounded it into a smooth oval, except for a dent on the far side that exposed its porous core. The ant finishes its cautious circumnavigation of the pebble and scurries slowly toward the arm, which lies across its path. With infinite patience, the ant begins to climb up the arm, slipping on the slick, mud-spattered fabric. The ant works its way down the arm to the wrist and stops, sampling the air. The ant stands among the bristly black hairs on the wrist, antennae vibrating. The big blue vein in the wrist can be seen under its tiny feet. The ant continues to walk up the wrist, pushing its way through the bristly hair, climbing onto the hand and walking purposefully through the hollow of the thumb. Slowly, it disappears around the knuckle of the first finger—

And I remember a day when I was in the first year of high school and my voice was changing and I was starting to grow hair in unusual places and I was sitting in English class and I wasn't paying too much attention even though I'm usually pretty good in English because I was in love with the girl who sat in front of me. I remember that she had long legs and soft brown hair and a laugh like a bell and the sun was coming in the window behind her and the sunlight made the downy hair on the back of her neck glow very faintly and I wanted to touch it with my fingertips and I wanted to undo the knot that held her hair to the top of her head and I wanted her hair to cascade down over my face soft against my skin and cover me and with the sunlight I could see the strap of her bra underneath her thin dress and I wanted to slide my fingers underneath it and unhook it and stroke her velvety skin. I remember that I could feel my body stirring and my mouth was dry and painful and the zipper of her dress was open a tiny bit at the top and I could see the tanned texture of her skin and see that she had a brown mole on her shoulder and my hand trembled with the urge to touch it and something about Shakespeare and when she turned her head to whisper to

Denny across the row her eyes were deep and beautiful and I wanted to kiss them softly brush them lightly as a bird's wing and Hamlet was something or other and I caught a glimpse of her tongue darting wetly from between her lips and pressing against her white teeth and that was almost too much to bear and I wanted to kiss her lips very softly and then I wanted to crush them flat and then I wanted to bite them and sting them until she cried and I could comfort and soothe her and that frightened me because I didn't understand it and my thighs were tight and prickly and the blood pounded at the base of my throat and Elsinore something and the bell rang shrilly and I couldn't get up because all I could see was the fabric of her dress stretched taut over her hips as she stood up and I stared at her hips and her belly and her thighs as she walked away and wondered what her thing would look like and I was scared. I remember that I finally got up enough nerve to ask her for a date during recess and she looked at me incredulously for a second and then laughed, just laughed contemptuously for a second and walked away without saying a word. I remember her laughter. And I remember wandering around town late that night heading aimlessly into nowhere trying to escape from the pressure and the emptiness and passing a car parked on a dark street corner just as the moon swung out from behind a cloud and there was light that danced and I could hear the freight trains booming far away and she was in the back seat with Denny and they were locked together and her skirt was hiked up and I could see the white flash of flesh all the way up her leg and he had his hand under her blouse on her breast and I could see his knuckles moving under the fabric and the freight train roared and clattered as it hit the switch and he was kissing her and biting her and she was kissing him back with her lips pressed tight against her teeth and her hair floating all around them like a cloud and the train was whispering away from town and then he was on top of her pressing her down and I felt like I was going to be sick and I started to vomit but stopped because I was afraid of the noise and she was moaning and making small low whimpering noises I'd never heard anyone make before and I had to run before the darkness crushed me and I didn't want to do that when I got home because I'd feel ashamed and disgusted afterward but I knew that I was going to have to because my stomach was heaving and my skin was on fire and I thought that my heart was going to explode. And I remember that I eventually got a date for the dance with Judy from my history class who was a nice girl although plain but all night long as I danced with her I could only see my first love moaning and writhing under Denny just as the worm had writhed under the thrust of the garden spade into the wet dark earth long ago and as I ran toward home that night I heard the train vanish into the night trailing a cruelly arrogant whistle behind it until it faded to a memory and there was nothing left.

—The ant reappears on the underside of the index finger, pauses, antennae flickering inquisitively, and then begins to walk back down the palm, following the deep groove known as the life line until it reaches the wrist. For a moment, it appears as if the ant will vanish into the space between the wrist and the frayed, bloodstained cuff of the shirt, but it changes its mind and slides back down the wrist to the ground on the far side. The ant struggles for a moment in the sticky mud, and then crawls determinedly off across the crusted ground. At the extreme edge of the field of vision, just before the blur that is the upper arm, there is the jagged, pebbly edge of a shellhole. Half over the lip of the shellhole, grossly out of proportion at this distance, is half of a large earthworm, partially buried by the freshly turned earth thrown up by an explosion. The ant pokes suspiciously at the worm—

And I remember the waiting room at the train station and the weight of my suitcase in my hand and the way the big iron voice rolled unintelligibly around the high ceiling as the stationmaster announced the incoming trains and cigar and cigarette smoke was thick in the air and the massive air-conditioning fan was laboring in vain to clear some of the choking fog away and the place reeked of urine and age and an old dog twitched and moaned in his ancient sleep as he curled close against an equally ancient radiator that hissed and panted and belched white jets of steam and I stood by the door and looked up and watched a blanket of heavy new snow settle down over the sleeping town with the ponderous invulnerability of a pregnant woman. I remember looking down into the train tunnel and out along the track to where the shining steel disappeared into darkness and I suddenly thought that it looked like a magic cave and then I wondered if I had thought that was supposed to be funny and I wanted to laugh only I wanted to cry too and so I could do neither and instead I tightened my arm around Judy's waist and pulled her closer against me and kissed the silken hollow of her throat and I could feel the sharp bone in her hip jabbing against mine and I didn't care because that was pain that was pleasure and I felt the gentle resilience of her breast suddenly against my rib cage and felt her arm tighten protectively around me and her fingernails bite sharply into my arm and I knew that she was trying not to cry and that if I said anything at all it would make her cry and there would be that sloppy scene we'd been trying to avoid and so I said nothing but only held her and kissed her lightly on the eyes and I knew that people were looking at us and snickering and I didn't give a damn and I knew that she wanted me and wanted me to stay and we both knew that I couldn't and all around us about ten other young men were going through similar tableaux with their girlfriends or folks and everybody was stern and pale and worried and trying to look unconcerned and casual and so many women were trying not to cry that the humidity in the station was trembling at the saturation point. I remember Denny standing near the door with a foot propped on his suitcase and he was flashing his too-white teeth and his too-wide smile and he reeked of cheap cologne as he told his small knot of admirers in an overly loud voice that he didn't give a damn if he went or not because he'd knocked up a broad and her old man was tryin to put the screws on him and this was a good way to get outta town anyway and the government would protect him from the old man and he'd come back in a year or so on top of the world and the heat would be off and he could start collectin female scalps again and besides his father had been in and been a hero and he could do anything better than that old bastard and besides he hated those goddamned Gooks and he was gonna get him a Commie see if he didn't. I remember that the train came quietly in then and that it still looked like a big iron beast although now it was a silent beast with no smoke or sparks but with magic still hidden inside it although I knew now that it might be a dark magic and then we had to climb inside and I was kissing Judy good-bye and telling her I loved her and she was kissing me and telling me that she would wait for me and I don't know if we were telling the truth or even if we knew ourselves what the truth was and then Judy was crying openly and I was swallowed by the iron beast and we were roaring away from the town and snickering across the web of tracks and booming over the switches and I saw my old house flash by and I could see my old window and I almost imagined that I could see myself as a kid with my nose pressed against the window looking out and watching my older self roar by and neither of us suspecting that the other was there and neither ever working up enough nerve to watch the trains dance. And I remember that all during that long train ride I could hear Denny's raucous voice somewhere in the distance talking about how he couldn't wait to get to Gookland and he'd heard that Gook snatch was even better than nigger snatch and free too and he was gonna get him a Commie he couldn't wait to get him a goddamned Commie and as the train slashed across the wide fertile farmlands of the Midwest the last thing I knew before sleep that night was the wet smell of freshly turned earth.

—The ant noses the worm disdainfully and then passes out of the field of vision. The only movement now is the ripple of the tall grass and the flash of birds in the shaggy tree. The sky is clouding up again, thunderheads rumbling up over the horizon and rolling across the sky. Two large forms appear near the shaggy tree at the other extreme of the field of vision. The singing of the birds stops as if turned off by a switch. The two forms move about vaguely near the shaggy tree, rustling the grass. The angle of the field of vision gives a foreshortening effect, and it is difficult to make out just what the figures are. There is a sharp command, the human voice sounding strangely thin under the sighing of the wind. The two figures move away from the shaggy tree, pushing through the grass. They are medics; haggard, dirty soldiers with big red crosses painted on their helmets and armbands and several days' growth on their chins. They look tired, harried, scared and determined, and they are moving rapidly, half-crouching, searching for something on the ground and darting frequent wary glances back over their shoulders. As they approach they seem to grow larger and larger, elongating toward the sky as their movement shifts the perspective. They stop a few feet away and reach down, lifting up a body that has been hidden by the tall grass. It is Denny, the back of his head blown away, his eyes bulging horribly open. The medics lower Denny's body back into the sheltering grass and bend over it, fumbling with something. They finally straighten, glance hurriedly about and move forward. The two grimy figures swell until they fill practically the entire field of vision, only random patches of the sky and the ground underfoot visible around their bulk, The medics come to a stop about a foot away. The scarred, battered, mud-caked combat boot of the medic now dominates the scene, looking big as a mountain. From the combat boot, the medic's leg seems to stretch incredibly toward the sky, like a fatigue-swathed beanstalk, with just a suggestion of a head and a helmet floating somewhere at the top. The other medic cannot be seen at all now, having stepped over and out of the field of vision. His shallow breathing and occasional muttered obscenities can be heard. The first medic bends over, his huge hand seeming to leap down from the sky, and touches the arm, lifting the wrist and feeling for a pulse. The medic holds the wrist for a while and then sighs and lets it go. The wrist plops limply back into the cold sucking mud, splattering it. The medic's hand swells in the direction of the upper arm, and then fades momentarily out of the field of vision, although his wrist remains barely visible and his arm seems to stretch back like a highway into the middle distance. The medic tugs, and his hand comes back clutching a tarnished dog tag. Both of the medic's hands disappear forward out of the field of vision. Hands prying the jaw open, jamming the dog tag into the teeth, the metal cold and slimy against the tongue and gums, pressing the jaws firmly closed again, the dog tag feeling huge and immovable inside the mouth. The world is the medic's face now, looming like a scarred cliff inches away, his bloodshot twitching eyes as huge as moons, his mouth, hanging slackly open with exhaustion, as

cavernous and bottomless as a magic cave to a little boy. The medic has halitosis, his breath filled with the richly corrupt smell of freshly turned earth. The medic stretches out two fingers which completely occupy the field of vision, blocking out even the sky. The medic's fingertips are the only things in the world now. They are stained and dirty and one has a white scar across the whorls. The medic's fingertips touch the eyelids and gently press down. And now there is nothing but darkness—

And I remember the way dawn would crack the eastern sky, the rosy blush slowly spreading and staining the black of night, chasing away the darkness, driving away the stars. And I remember the way a woman looks at you when she loves you, and the sound that a kitten makes when it is happy, and the way that snowflakes blur and melt against a warm windowpane in winter. I remember. I remember.

We're glad to welcome Nigerian writer Walter Dinjos to the pages of Galaxy's Edge. *His other appearances include* Beneath Ceaseless Skies, Deep Magic, Lamplight, *and more.*

BEING A GIANT IN MEN'S WORLD

by Walter Dinjos

Our neighbors said that when the doctor carved me out of Mama's belly, the midwives all scrambled out of the maternity ward screaming abomination, their hands on their heads. They gossiped that I didn't only arrive the size and weight of two average babies, but also had four fingers on each hand and two teeth protruding from the roof of my mouth.

The next month, the hospital became so unpopular that it closed down due to bankruptcy. Apparently no one wanted to lie on the same bed that delivered a monstrosity.

Although I don't remember any of this, and I have ten fingers—mama said the teeth part of the gossip is true—it appears my life started to fall apart the moment I stepped into this pathetic world of men. It wasn't until my teenagehood, however, that I began to realize this. The signs became too jarring to ignore.

For instance, I remember my last day at Model Central Secondary School when Principal Eji expelled me simply because I shooed some pesky rascals away from my teenage crush, Nenye. I overheard the boys plotting at the back of the classroom to lure her into the savannah thicket behind the chaplaincy and molest her—that's the thing about having big ears; everything, even the slightest whisper, funnels in—and I had to do something about it.

But then Nenye and her buffoon of a mother supported my expulsion, claiming I assaulted the boys who were all a little over five feet. I, on the other hand, was seven-feet tall and my feet were at least twice the size of theirs. I suppose that when someone gets so big in stature, common sense suggests that everyone would avoid picking a fight with him. Thus, any fight he engages in must have been picked by him.

Then there was the many times Mama had to reconstruct our doors and windows and raise our roof to accommodate my height. She had to work four jobs to earn enough money for the regular reconstruction while I managed the farm. She didn't know how tall I was going to get, so she kept predicting and rebuilding.

Once I asked her who my father was. Instead of an answer, she lulled me to sleep with tales of her adventures in the giant snake-ridden Asho Forest about a hundred miles from town. She said the reptiles, contrary to what people believe, aren't aggressive except when faced with human invasion.

"So far they've kept wood cutters at bay and the forest preserved," she said. "That's a good thing, isn't it?"

I nodded and dozed off in my then three meters long hay bed. Now it's five meters long.

If someone told me I'd one day lose her, I would probably grab the person and break him in two. She was all I had. She kept me hidden and safe from the world, schooled me at home when no secondary school would admit me, and toiled to satisfy my ever-growing stomachOften I would sit in the parlor and stare at the picture we took together, the one hanging over the black-and-white television the same age as me. We were both eighteen then—the television and me. It was a fourteen-inch box and I was eleven feet tall and, in the picture above it, I carried Mama in one arm. I remember the photographer had trembled as he took the shot, and the next day he had called Mama and asked her to come to his office and collect the picture. Alone.

Now that she's gone, I always carry that framed picture in my big trouser pocket. Comfortably. Being a giant, it seems, has its perks. Just two perks, I think. The other one presented itself the day my uncles arrived to take over Mama's properties. They came wearing red hats adorned with vulture feathers and palm fronds to show that the old gods were with them. As soon as they saw me, they changed their minds and recoiled out of our compound.

Thus I was left alone, without the love and care of a mother. Not that a twenty-year-old needs a mother to survive, but knowing the world out there with its politics, inequality, and unfairness, as Mama portrayed it, I couldn't get myself to go outside. I fed on our barn of yam, rice, and beans. Then I moved over to the livestock until soon all I had left was the two-hundred-thousand naira in Mama's micro-wave-sized piggy bank.

And I reckoned I ought to go out into the world and live life like everyone else. It was time to break out of the comfort of our high fences. To do that, I figured I needed a few things. A mobile phone was the most important—I bought a tablet instead; yes, because I'm a giant and because punching the tiny buttons on Mama's phone was frustrating.

✿

Last week I saw a poster indicating vacancy in a company called Chibex Haulage and Logistics. Since the word "haulage" was included in the company's name—logistics seemed too complicated to think about—and the vacant position, as stated on the poster, was "delivery manager," I figured I, with my extravagant stoutness, would fit right in. These big muscular hands of mine have worked my mother's farm for ten years, and that involved a lot of hauling and dumping. There was no one more qualified for the job.

I only wished the bald interviewer agreed. I think he would have agreed had he actually interviewed me.

A lot of things went wrong that day. No, now that I think of it, only one thing went wrong that day, and it is the fact that I'm a giant. You must understand that there is a difference between a tall person and a giant, and it is that the latter has more balance because his body parts are more proportionally distributed. So what's the problem here?

Has anyone ever gone for a job interview only to realize he or she can't have the job because he or she is a dwarf—you see what I did there? Of course, that never happens; the interviewer was below five feet, I swear. And I think that was the problem. Jealousy. Inferiority complex. Low self-esteem. He must have felt all that when he ambled outside to call me in.

The first thing he did was look me over from head to toe—I imagined that took a bit of straining in the neck—and regard the seven-feet-high door behind him which can attest to his dwarfism. I could picture him wondering how a fifteen-feet-tall giant was going to fit through that door.

"Man, you are tall. You are a man, right?" he finally said.

To that I said nothing, since a website I visited the previous night suggested "being on one's best behavior" as one of the prerequisites of a successful job interview—not that I couldn't stamp him to death if I wanted to.

"But no vacancy for you," he added.

His words infused my heart with much sadness that there was no space left for anger. I'm a human being too, am I not? Why couldn't they reconstruct their office doors and roof just like Mama did our home? I'm a human being and door makers and house builders ought to consider that not everybody is just six feet tall.

As I slouched out of the company's bungalow-filled compound, I resisted the urge to grab the interviewer, lift him up, shake him up both with my hands and my stare and bellow into his small ears that I was more qualified for any hauling job than those short idiots he let in. But then I was certain he'd have said, "How can you be? I don't see any schools with fifteen-feet-high doors around. Do you?"

I trekked home that afternoon with two big bottles of kai kai trapped in my armpits. If you are looking to drink yourself out of, or even into, misery, that's the name to ask for in your local liquor store. But if your problems are the size of Jupiter or, worse, anything like mine, then add a bottle of palm wine to it, as I did, and you'll sleep off for at least three days.

Well, I didn't sleep for three days. My giant immune system shook the alcohol off in just three hours. Wait, is it the immune system that shakes drunkenness off? Or is it the head, as in the brain? I ask this because folk around here often say, "His head no strong enough to handle the liquor," to men that pass out after a bottle. Plus, I woke up with a little lightness in the *head*. See? "Head" everywhere.

That light-headedness and the accompanying hangover was what made me stumble along my dingy neighborhood looking for a girl to woo. I settled for the first one I bumped into. She was tall, at least six feet tall, and her orange-ish skin was riddled with tiny dark spots.

She was respectful, I think, considering that she stopped when I said, "Excuse me." Not many people would do that for me. But there was something about the way she contemplated me, as if she was wondering how awkward our first kiss was going to be, seeing as I would have to really bend or scoop her up to kiss her and I might end up licking her nose with my large lips and tongue. Either that or she was imagining how my stuff was going to fit in hers when we got down to intimacy. I thought they said that women liked it big.

It was when she began to stammer and back away that I realized I had more problems as a giant than I thought. So I stumbled home, wept through the night, and decided to try online dating the following day. My tablet came in handy in this case. The app I used was called Introverted Dating, and since it forced users to resize their pictures after uploading them, my face was the only part of me that went live on my profile.

I quickly messaged a few ladies. One replied. And she was in Awka. So we arranged to meet at Ms. K's Joint at Unizik Junction.

It was on our date that I discovered that the taller you get, the fewer and uglier the women in your dating pool. I mean, the four-feet-tall actor, Aku, is dating the current Miss Nigeria. Contrary to what they say, women like it small, it seems.

I strutted into Ms. K's Joint at exactly five p.m. that day. The place was a bush bar, roofs high and made of raffia, seats made of woven palm fiber, and tables made of trunks and stone. That was why I had chosen the place—no doors; lots of open space. My date, Uche, was already sitting by a mud pool and was all togged up as if she was there for a wedding reception. She was tall, taller and uglier than most of the men in the bar.

As I walked up to her, slowly so that my flip-flopped feet didn't make the ground tremble, she looked behind me as if to check whether I had a bodyguard. No, I think she checked to see if I was the bodyguard. I presume because when you are guarding someone, sometimes the best place to stand is at the person's front—that's if the threat approaches from there.

When she saw no one behind me, and my hand was already descending for a handshake, she screamed, "Jesus!" and ran with her koi koi shoes in her hands.

The manager of the joint, who was as slim as a snake and dressed like a hungry banker, immediately called security for me. I explained that I came for a date, and he said, "Oh. We are sorry for this misunderstanding, but I think you may have chosen the wrong restaurant." His bulging eyes indicated the seat beside us as if asking without words, "Do you want to break it?" The people dining around us stared at me with great unease. A man had his mouth open, a spoonful of fried rice hanging before it as though he was in a television show and someone decided to touch the pause button.

✿

I'm fed up. I'm outraged. And I've decided that the world needs to know about the unfairness in the way they treat me. I need to put it out there, right in their faces and ask them to do something about it. I'm a human being too. I'm Nigerian too and I have rights.

So I make a placard using one wing of our barn door and the leftover paint from Mama's last reconstruction of the house. The placard reads, GIANTS ARE HUMANS TOO. GIANTS ARE NIGERIAN TOO, and I carry it down to the front of Government House along the Enugu-Onitsha Expressway, and air my grievances via a megaphone I borrowed from our neighborhood beggar—it is true that the less privileged are the most accommodating people in Nigeria.

It doesn't take long and people begin to gather. I smile. They are listening. Perhaps tomorrow I'll partake in another job interview.

An old woman limps up to me. I think she means to hug me. That would be reassuring, even though her face is heavily wrinkled.

"What are you doing?" she asks. The cacophony of impatient drivers honking and curious bystanders muttering drowns her words, but my big ears are able to fish them out from that sea of noise.

"Protesting," I say.

"Alone? Don't you need more giants in order to pull this sort of thing off?"

I feel a sudden wave of shame. The people watching me aren't listening, I realize. They are laughing in their hearts at a boneheaded giant making a nuisance out of himself. My eyes comb my surroundings. I've caused a serious traffic jam.

The police, thirteen men in charcoal black uniforms, arrive with heavy guns. If I weren't the one they came for, I'd have definitely concluded that there were armed terrorists in the area and they meant to invade Government House. I suppose the policemen imagined that since I dwarf them all, I could put up a hell of a fight. And that's what the guns are for.

They try to handcuff me, but the cuffs are much too small for my wrists. Dejected, I follow them, willingly, and as I climb onto the back of their Tundra, the vehicle groans and slumps.

I don't think they've thought this thing through because if they have, they would have realised beforehand that their cells were built for men and not giants. That realization comes to them when we reach their station at Amawbia Junction. And with sighs on their lips and frowns on their faces, they let me go.

I smile all the way as I jog home. Being a giant is not so bad.

✿

The next morning, I wake up, tune the television to NTA Channel 5, and find myself on the seven o'clock news.

Black-and-white televisions, it appears, aren't too small to accommodate me. Unlike doors, they don't discriminate. They accommodate everyone.

Governor Ebube speaks on the news about placing me on a monthly salary. But that's not what I want. Of course, I'd relish the free money, but I just want to work, earn, meet a girl, live like a normal human, a normal Nigerian.

I turn off the television and recline on our massive sofa and pray that my brief fame fetches me a girl that likes giants. When I get a heavy knock on my door, I leap up and tug at my sleeves and slacks to straighten them up where they are rumpled in case the knock is my prayer being answered.

Instead, I open the door to find a man…a giant much taller and broader than me standing outside in the company of an equally imposing steed.

"I've come to take you home, son," he says.

"Home?" The word that sticks with me is the other one—*son*.

"The Asho Forest."

Copyright © 2018 by Walter Dinjos

Leah Cypess has sold stories to Asimov's, Fantasy & Science Fiction, Daily Science Fiction, *and other markets. She is also the author of four fantasy novels, starting with* Mistwood, *and has been a Nebula nominee. This is her first appearance in* Galaxy's Edge.

CHOCOLATE CHIP COOKIES WITH LOVE POTION INFUSION

by Leah Cypess

About me:
Heather
Proud witch, baker, and blogger

After a *lot* of trial and error, I have finally perfected these cookies—a fun modern twist on love potions. They taste amazing, plus they totally work. Ask me how I know!! :) :)

I used **this** recipe from BakerMomma as a starter, with a few variations:

As a substitute for the corn syrup, I used 1 teaspoon organic molasses mixed with 1/2 tablespoon organic honey, 1/4 tablespoon organic brown sugar, and 1/4 tablespoon plus 3 drops organic water.

For the oil I used ~~canola oil~~ ~~grapeseed oil~~ coconut oil.

Last but not least, I added 1/8 cup chia seeds. If you love someone enough to put a spell on him, wouldn't you also want to help him get the toxins out of his body?

And now, for the magical ingredients! Make sure to follow these instructions *exactly*:

Three hairs from your beloved. The *Witch Goddess Bloggess* recommends direct plucking as a method of obtaining this ingredient to best avoid mix-ups (apparently, this was the cause of the Brad Pitt/Angelina Jolie romance). Based on personal experience, I really cannot recommend this. Instead, try to obtain hair from a hairbrush or hat. If you're lucky, like me, you have a platonic guy friend who can help you with that.

Two teaspoons fresh human blood. I recommend using your own to avoid mix-ups and possible jail time.

Eye of newt. Fresh ones are pricey, but they really brighten up this recipe. You can use freeze-dried eye of newt, but I find it has an artificial, chemically taste. Nevertheless, if you don't have refined taste buds and/or you've made poor financial decisions in your life, the freeze-dried variety is worth a try.

Five four-leaf clovers gathered in moonlight while chanting prayers to a goddess.

1/8 cup rainwater gathered at dawn while walking counterclockwise and singing songs from Hamilton.

1/4 cup crushed bone. *Human* bone is ideal, and I was almost able to use it—my friend Stephen, who is pre-med, thought he could get me some. In the end, I had to settle for chicken bone.

INSTRUCTIONS

1. Mix all magical ingredients, except crushed bone, in a large stone basin that has never been touched by anything made in China. Add mundane ingredients.

2. Bake at 350 degrees for 20 minutes, or until lightly browned on top.

3. Convince your beloved to accompany you to the shore of a body of water at sunset.

4. This part can be difficult. I ended up having to drug my beloved a little bit and drag him to the university's fish pond. Luckily, my friend Stephen was willing to help. Hopefully, the chia seeds will repair whatever damage the drugs did my beloved's body. And yes, I do feel guilty, but let's be honest: he plays football. These are not the first drugs his body has encountered.

5. Sprinkle ground bone over the surface of the water.

6. Have your beloved eat at least three cookies. (Difficult to do while drugged, as I discovered. Stephen's medical experience came in handy here.)

7. Put on lipstick (optional) and enjoy some undying affection!

What do you guys think? Let me know when you've tried it—I can't wait to hear about some happy endings!

RATE & COMMENT

Circe ★ ★ ★

I find this really disturbing. Coconut oil is full of the wrong kind of fat and has a high melting point (or a low one? I forget which, but it's bad). You should be using hemp seed oil in all your recipes, as I do.

I also halved the molasses (except I used honey) and substituted half whole-wheat flour and half almond flour. I couldn't taste the difference, and it seems to be working really well. Do you have a counterspell?

Heather I'm working on it.
Circe Please hurry.

Hermione ★ ★

Very bland. Could have used a dash of something—maybe cinnamon or nutmeg. The cookies did work, but I have to say, sometimes it's better to admire gorgeousness from afar than to have to make conversation with it.

Heather LOL, I'm starting to see your point. (About the gorgeousness. Not about the spices. Just to be clear.)
Hermione Please update when you have that counterspell recipe.

Anonymous ★ ★ ★ ★

I hate to say it, but Stephen sounds like a way better catch than Football Guy.

Heather Somehow, I doubt you hate to say that, *Anonymous.*
Anonymous Well, I hate that I *have* to say it.
Heather Haha. I think Amanda would hate hearing you say it too.
Anonymous Ouch. Touché.

Polgara ★ ★ ★

I substituted animal blood for the human blood, regular clovers for the four-leaf clovers, and left out the chia seeds. The cookies taste fine, but they don't seem to be working. What a waste of good ingredients.

Glinda ✴ ✴ ✴ ✴

I don't know why people completely change a recipe and then review it. Why bother? Go invent your own recipe and leave Heather alone. I made this exactly as written and it was delicious.

Amanda ✴

I'm not really into witchcraft, but this looked so intriguing, I had to give it a try. They are pretty good, though I wish you'd included nutrition information—I cannot find the calorie content of human blood *anywhere*. But I tried these cookies on my boyfriend and they didn't work. Does that mean he really is incapable of love? My therapist thinks my making the cookies in the first place is the bigger issue and refuses to discuss anything else.

Amanda So it turns out my boyfriend realized what I did and only faked eating the cookies. Apparently, he reads this blog. He knows all about this spell. Isn't that creepy? I'm clearly better off without him.

Circe I find it ironic that this comes right after your post about changing your major to intersectional non-Western feminism. Don't you find this a bit hypocritical?

Heather Love spells empower women. Hating on love spells is sexist and patriarchal.

Circe I'd feel a lot more empowered if there was an antidote.

Heather I'M WORKING ON IT. Everyone stop messaging me, please.

Hermione Question, do you think it's *extra* unethical to cheat on someone after you've bound them to love you forever?

Heather I've been thinking about that recently. At first I thought yes, but now I think that's just conventional morality bound up in societal sexism. According to my research, the witches of old had no problem keeping multiple lovers enthralled by their spells.

Hermione The witches of old also had no problem killing their lovers and grinding up their bones.

Heather Yeah. I've been thinking about that too.

Willow ✴

I cannot believe all the positive reviews. These were inedible. I had to give them to my dogs. Who, by the way, have shown no change in behavior whatsoever.

Lilith I stumbled across this post while doing research for my dissertation. According to everything I've read, there is no antidote to this spell

Circe WHAT?

Glinda WTF.

Hermione There has got to be an antidote. There. Has. Got. To. Be.

Circe *Sobbing emoji*

Hermione *Sobbing-*er* emoji*

Glinda *Sobbing emoji that for some reason is a sobbing penguin dancing on a turtle*

Lilith Sorry, guys. My computer shut down when I was in middle of typing. There's no antidote *but* a later spell will cancel out a former spell. So if you can get someone else to put a spell on your beloved, that will erase the effects of the original spell.

Amanda Wow, can't believe the last comment was three months ago! Just an update, you can use flaxseed instead of chia. Gives the cookies a chewier flavor, and the potion still works.

Hermione You have your boyfriend back?

Amanda Haha no. That loser had a crush on someone else all along. But my new guy is seven times hotter than him *and* a football player. They make more money than doctors do, anyhow.

Circe Does the antidote work the opposite way around? If I have someone else do the spell on me, will that cancel out the spell I did on my beloved?

Anonymous Sorry, no. It will make you fall in love with whoever gives you the potion, but it won't affect your beloved.

Circe How do you know?

Heather Good question, *Anonymous*. HOW DO YOU KNOW?

Anonymous Sorry, can't type now—I'm in chem lab. Let's talk tonight, okay? I'll meet you at our usual place.

Heather You mean next to Bear Creek?

Anonymous Yup. See you there.

Copyright © 2018 by Leah Cypess

Kij Johnson is a Hugo winner and a multiple Nebula winner. Her most recent novel is The River Bank. *We're happy to welcome her back to the pages of* Galaxy's Edge.

CHENTING, IN THE LAND OF THE DEAD

by Kij Johnson

In the end, the only job that presented itself was the governorship of a remote province in the land of the dead. Chenting was the name of the place, and the scholar and his concubine, Ah Lien, talked of it often as they lay entangled in their sweaty robes after lovemaking.

It would be a place of fields, he said. The peasants will farm rice and raise oxen. The air will smell a bit like the smoke from the false money that is burned to give one influence among the dead; but it will also be rich with perfumes, the scents that only dogs and pigs can smell in this world.

No, she said. It shall be like distant Tieling, where the fields lead up to the mountains, except that the mountains will never stop but will go up and up; and gray snow shall blow like dust across the fields, and the sky will be the purple-black of a thundercloud's heart or a marten's wing. And it will be lonely, she said, and held him tighter, pressing her face against his neck.

✿

He was dying; they both knew that. The man with the eyes of smoke, the man who had come to tell him of the post at Chenting, had said so.

"But I am waiting to hear how I performed at the examinations!" the scholar had said to him. "I was hoping for a position somewhere."

The man bowed as he had at the start of the conversation: as before, the bow seemed both perfunctory and punctilious. "And well you might hope. Hope is the refuge of the desperate. But please allow me to be candid here. You are poor, and cannot afford the bribes or fees for anything better than, let us say, a goatherdship. And this governorship in Chenting, in the land of the dead, is available immediately."

The scholar stroked his chin. "But I am not dead."

"You shall be soon enough," the man said. "It is as certain as, well, taxes."

The scholar frowned. "Are there no other candidates for this position that you seek a living man to fill it?"

"As I have said, you shall not live many months longer, making this point moot."

"Well then, are there other dead candidates?—Or soon to be dead," the scholar added.

"Well, yes, there are always candidates. But I feel sure that your qualifications shall prevail." The man with eyes of smoke made a gesture like two coins clinking together.

"But—" the scholar began and stopped. "I must consult."

The man bowed yet again and left.

"Well?" the scholar said to the empty room. There was a soft brushing of fabric and Ah Lien glided from behind the patched screen with the painted camellias. She was better than he deserved, the lovely Ah Lien, with eyes as narrow and long and green as willow leaves, better than he could afford, except that her birth was common and the eyes were considered a questionable asset for a woman in her position.

"You heard," he said. A statement, not a question. Of course she had heard. She was one ear, he was the other.

"Chenting," she whispered. "In the land of the dead. When must you leave, my lord?"

✿

And that was that. There was no choice about his dying, only about his position in the scheme of things after his death, and both knew it was better to be a dead governor than a dead scholar.

But he lingered for a time with her, and they talked often of Chenting.

The governor's palace, he said, will be built of white stone and then plastered over, so that even where the plaster has cracked the walls will glow like bleached silk. And the roof will be covered with ceramic tiles the color of daylilies. The gardens will have countless enclosed roofless areas, each filled with hanging baskets containing small pines whose needles chime when one passes.

No, she said, the gardens are cold and abandoned. Winds blow through the empty rooms, and sometimes one sits by an unglazed window, watching the patterns made by dead leaves blown in the air.

It cannot be like that, he said. It must be as I see it.

If it is, she murmured, summon me to your side and I will come.

✿

They had already decided she could not accompany him. The man with eyes like smoke had said nothing of her, and Ah Lien was understandably reluctant to die. She loved the scholar dearly but she had aging parents to consider and an ancestral shrine to tend. Still: she was willing.

✿

His death when it came was a comparatively simple one. He coughed a bit as the winter began to take hold. Ah Lien held him close and warmed him when chills shook him. Then they talked of Chenting.

The bedrooms of the governor's palace, he said, and paused to catch his breath. The bedrooms have braziers of porcelain shaped like horses, and each horse bears a silver saddle on its back, and each saddle holds a fire of charcoal. The smoke that curls up smells of sandalwood and jasmine. And the bed is soft, covered with silk, with pillows carved of black wood. And the pillow book there has positions we have never imagined.

No, she said, the beds at Chenting are cold and narrow and hard, made of wheat husks in hemp bags. The smoke smells of funeral biers, but the fires are cold and colored the blue of foxfire in the marshes at night. "Do not leave me, my love," she said.

"I will send for you," he promised, and died.

✿

When he awakened in Chenting he was amazed at first at how well he felt. There was no pain, no trouble breathing, no aches from holding a brush too tightly or walking in new shoes. And Chenting was everything he had imagined and more. The fields were lusher than he had expected and seemed to be near harvest. The air smelled as rich as he had dreamed. And he had much money to spend, for

Ah Lien had sold her hair ornaments to buy paper money, and burned it so that it would follow him.

He missed her and wanted her beside him, and since Chenting was warm and beautiful and not like the cold visions she had feared, he sent a message to her. "Come," it read. "I have seen Chenting and it is as fair as I envisioned. The birds are the colors of flames, and their songs are sharp as the crackling of fire. Come sit beside me." He sent a messenger off, with an entourage to show her the honor she deserved.

The messenger returned. "She is coming," he said.

✿

Many days later, the entourage at last arrived, brilliant with tassels, loud with flutes. The governor of Chenting straightened his cap and calmed his heart, and descended the red stairs leading to the courtyard where his entourage milled about the sedan chair he had sent for her. He brushed aside the chair's gold-thread curtain. "Ah Lien—" he began.

For an instant he heard Ah Lien sobbing, and then that was gone. The sedan chair was empty and silent.

The governor of Chenting stormed and raged and ordered great punishments for the entourage that had failed to keep her safe. But even as he wept and cursed, he knew what had happened.

He had found Chenting just as he had expected, a place where an old man's pains were eased. But she had imagined another Chenting, a place where youth is irrelevant and even beauty is lonely. He did not know the Chenting she had gone to, but he knew it was not his.

Copyright © 1999 by Kij Johnson

Brian K. Lowe is the author of more than thir-ty-five stories, as well as six novels (including the Stolen Future trilogy.) This is his first ap-pearance in Galaxy's Edge.

REALITY SHOW

by Brian K. Lowe

They dismantled Australia today. Just took it apart and packed it in trunks and carried it off to a warehouse somewhere. Theoretically, everybody had already left, but there's always some-body who doesn't leave, no matter what the disas-ter…fire, flood, storm… What happened to those people when the entire set that we called the South-ern Continent was struck and hauled away?

I don't really want to know.

I'm supposed to be having lunch with my agent today. I got a postcard in the mail. Well, in my mail-box, since there's no such thing as "mail" any more. It was addressed to me personally. How did they do that? Even with sixty percent of the human race dead or terminally insane, that still leaves over two billion of us. Who keeps track of who's alive, who's sane, and where we can be found?

And since when do I have *an agent*?

☼

"Marty! Sit down! It's good to finally meet you in person." My "agent," thin, hyperactive, a little bald on top, pointed me toward a cushy leather guest chair in a office lined with shelves full of Oscars, Emmys, Tonys, and Hugos. "Sit down, we got a lot to talk about." He held out a business card. "Sid Mandelbraum."

I held his card in my hand, but it didn't make him seem any more real. It sounded like he'd gotten his whole identity from watching cheap basic cable shows. Then I remembered—he had. One show in particular. It was called *Earth*.

"It was a good show, while it lasted," Sid was saying, irrespective of my paying any attention. "It had in-trigue, romance, and above all, lots of action. View-ers really like action shows. Most of them aren't into *taking* a whole lot of action these days, they're all, 'We're so evolved,' don'tcha know." His voice went low. "'We are beings of thought. We have forsaken our physical bodies.' Yeah, they're all so advanced all they want to do all day is watch 'lesser beings' trying to kill each other on a massive scale. Like us, am I right? If that's being 'evolved,'"—air quotes—"who needs it. Am I right? You know I'm right.

"But all good things must come to an end. I've seen it before; you jumped the shark when you started with that League of Nations stuff. I still had hopes you'd go out on your own terms, with a big, splashy finale, all ICBMs and pretty explosions… Oh, well, what's done is done, but if you've got to be cancelled, at least I can find some more work for a few of my fellow 'lesser beings.' Like you, Marty. Not one in a million has your gift—or your fan base."

"Fan base? What, you mean my blog?"

Sid threw back his head and guffawed. It was an ugly sound, and it reminded me that no matter what he looked like, Sid was not human.

"Marty, Marty, Marty. Your blog never had more than fourteen followers. Even your mother didn't read it. I'm talking about *fans. Viewers.* They love you! Well, they love to watch you… There are over eighteen billion beings out there who think you are one of the most annoying creatures in the multiverse. Granted, I thought you'd jumped the shark yourself when you started going to those anger management seminars, but you saved the day when you clocked your brother. Very dramatic. I almost cried."

I felt like I'd been kneecapped with a baseball bat. "Beings…watching me? Personally?"

Sid leaned over and gently slapped my face. "Yes, you. Personally. It's a reality show, remember? They've been watching you all your life. They're watching you right now. Your fans are on the edge of their seats waiting to see if you'll get your own show. They're taking bets in Vegas."

I held up a finger to stop him. "They packed up Vegas six months ago."

"Oh contrary, *mi amigo*. Multiversal Studios bought the whole town and licensed it to the An-dromeda Galaxy. Man, I wish that'd been my client. They got killer ratings. But hey, I got you."

"What do you mean, you've got me? Who gave me to you?"

"Marty, baby, you've got it all wrong. Nobody gave you to me, they gave me to you." He shrugged.

"Okay, maybe a little of both. I picked up your option when Earth was cancelled. Cost me a pretty penny too. But I know you're going to be worth it."

"You picked up my option? Like, from the people who did this to me? To us? To the entire planet? You *know* them?"

Sid looked up from his smart phone. "Well, I don't exactly *know* them, but we do business in the same circles. There were rumors Earth was about to be taken off, so I jumped in and started making some deals." He sat up straighter and took a conspiratorial look around. "To be honest, I did them a favor. If I hadn't come along and shown them there was still some value in the franchise, they would have just let it run straight into the ground. Another hundred years, you guys would have figured out how to work together to fix your problems. Pretty soon, bam! No more wars, no more territorial incursions—and no more ratings!"

I went from kneecapped to being punched in the solar plexus. "Are you saying," I croaked, "that if you, Sid Mandelbraum, hadn't stepped in, we would have eventually solved our problems? No more wars? No more pollution? No more—fighting?" My fingers began to clench spasmodically.

"Exactly, Marty, baby! No more fighting—utter disaster! The network would have dropped you like a hot latke!"

My breath was coming in gasps. "You destroyed the Earth for *ratings*!?" I jumped from the chair, grabbed a rocket-shaped Hugo, and smashed his smirking face, pounding him over and over and over again until I dropped the trophy, exhausted.

"You see?" Sid's voice burbled from the mess that had been his human skull. "That's what I'm talking about! The networks are going to *love* you!"

Copyright © 2018 by Brian K. Lowe

We're happy to welcome Brian Trent back to our pages. He has also appeared in Analog, Fantasy & Science Fiction, COSMOS, Nature, Escape Pod, Daily Science Fiction, *and more.*

JACKBOX

by Brian Trent

The dead body springs up from the sand, blindly jerks its service pistol at me, and squeezes the trigger. The rusty hammer comes down on an empty chamber but it keeps firing, the combat gloves contracting over and over across the grip. I freeze, staring into the corpse's howling, skeletal face. The mouth hangs open because the jaw muscles have rotted away. The eyes are likewise gone, yet the bitter cold of the Gobi has resulted in patchwork gray flesh—tough as leather—stretched tight across forehead and nose. It looks, I think, like an especially macabre party mask.

Click! Click! Click! Click!

My legs give out, my chest burns, as if there had indeed been a round in the dead man's chamber. I collapse backward against a mound of sand.

The howling dead man keeps trying to kill me. His arm is rigid, sand spilling from the cuff of his sleeve in a long, slow, *hisssssssssss*.

Jackbox.

I'd never seen one up close before, and suddenly the old joke in the barracks isn't the least bit funny. *We're all potential jackboxes now! Death can't stop you from fighting the good fight!*

Click! Click! Click!

I try crawling backward to put distance between myself and the dead man's postmort sensors. Who knew how long ago he had died, but his combat suit batteries still have juice in them, and the invisible tripwire of his sensors remains functional. The servos in his combat gloves keep contracting, his dead finger squeezing the trigger in relentless succession. The howling corpse is beyond reasoning, but his postmort circuitry can detect a foreign soldier. It *knows* I'm his enemy.

Sitting across from him, fear still burning a hole in my chest, I appraise my would-be executioner.

There are no visible wounds in his skeleton face, no damage to his chestplate or stiffened arm greaves or endlessly spasming combat glove. The fellow is buried in sand to the waist. Maybe his mortal wound is below the belt. Maybe a supply truck ran him over, or perhaps—more grimly—he had stepped on a sand-mine and gone cartwheeling through the sky to flop about like a ragdoll until coming to rest here, in this spot, where weeks or months later I happened to be walking by on reconnaissance.

Click! Click! Click! Click!

Whatever grim calculus had allowed me to cross the invisible tripwire of his sensors had also seen fit to ensure that he had no bullets left in his service pistol. That would have been terrible luck indeed, to get shot by a corpse a week before I go home for holiday leave. *Hi Mom! You know how I wrote that I'm looking forward to a home-cooked spaghetti meal? Sorry, but I have to cancel. Skeletor got me.*

Except that didn't happen. What *will* happen is that I will stand up and make a cautious retreat. His dead arm will continue tracking me until his postmort sensors determine the threat audit has moved off, and then the arm will lower, and a renewed gush of sand will pour from the sleeve. In another couple days, the ever-shifting desert will consume him again.

Fighting a war over sand, Mom said the night before I shipped out. She knows that the endless construction booms of the arcologies require sand for their dizzying development projects. *Next we'll be reverting to building ziggurats again with mud and straw. Then what? Cave paintings? Fighting over ochre dyes?*

I want to stand up—I mean, the desire is there—but something holds me in place. What if there are other jackboxes about? What if I'm sitting amid a hidden graveyard of the mechanically undead? If I make a wrong move, other bodies might burst out like trapdoor spiders. Jackbox!

My face flushes in sudden, unexpected guilt.

Jackbox?

Skeletor?

This soldier across from me must have a name. It's not visible on his armor the way mine is; if somebody finds me they'll see *my* name in black letters: PVT TROPASSO. Maybe I should check for the guy's dog tags or mercenary company tattoo. Maybe when this war is all over—

You mean when we find something else to fight for? Mom asks in my head.

I'll try contacting his family. Because how else will they know what happened to *their* son or husband or father out here? The desert is a protean predator, roving about in ceaseless, million-year patterns. My opposite number might easily vanish into the dunes again, emerging in some future epoch when the wind resculpts the desert, old sensors stirring beneath the sun's touch like some deep space probe stuck in the crevice of an alien world coming back to life for a few minutes every year, as the planet's axial tilt is like a gentleman's bow, imbuing it with a brief spark of life.

Click! Click! Click!

I remember apocryphal tales of WWII Japanese soldiers emerging from the Philippine jungle years after peace was declared, still thinking a war was on. Once I *get up off my ass* I'll leave this revenant behind and maybe years later some hapless sand-hunter will pass this way with his mechanical vacuums when all of a sudden the dead soldier—

Click!

—is exhumed by accident.

A pasta dinner, please, I emailed my parents. *Great heaping mounds of spaghetti and red sauce that I'll smell from the sidewalk.*

And Mom, in her trademark all-caps style, had replied: *COME HOME SAFE TO US.*

I will, Mom. It won't be my bad luck to get killed by the last remaining round in the pistol of a corpse. That punch to my chest, that sudden jab, was only my nerves.

Click! Click! Click!

I really should get up now, but I'm so tired and the sand has turned to red mud around me. Really shouldn't sleep here. It's too cold. Too lonely.

Too hard to move.

Except that I *am* moving suddenly. My pistol arm rises, taking aim at the howling corpse. But I shouldn't do that! He's not a threat to anyone. It's not necessary to—

My gloves spasm and the shot blows out the back of his skull. The next round hits him in his howling mouth and the teeth burst like potsherds.

I empty an entire clip into him.
Click!
Click!
Click!
It's cold, Mommy. That's the sound you hear.
My teeth must be chattering…

Copyright © 2018 by Brian Trent

*Joe Haldeman is a multiple Hugo and Nebula Award winner, the author of an acknowledged classic (*The Forever War*), and a former World-con Guest of Honor. We're proud to welcome him back to the pages of* Galaxy's Edge. *We should also mention that "None So Blind" is a Hugo winner.*

NONE SO BLIND

by Joe Haldeman

It all started when Cletus Jefferson asked himself, "Why aren't all blind people geniuses?" Cletus was only thirteen at the time, but it was a good question, and he would work on it for fourteen more years, and then change the world forever.

Young Jefferson was a polymath, an autodidact, a nerd literally without peer. He had a chemistry set, a microscope, a telescope, and several computers, some of them bought with paper route money. Most of his income was from education, though: teaching his classmates not to draw to inside straights.

Not even nerds, not even nerds who are poker players nonpareil, not even nerdish poker players who can do differential equations in their heads, are immune to Cupid's darts and the sudden storm of testosterone that will accompany those missiles at the age of thirteen. Cletus knew that he was ugly and his mother dressed him funny. He was also short and pudgy and could not throw a ball in any direction. None of this bothered him until his duct-less glands started cooking up chemicals that weren't in his chemistry set.

So Cletus started combing his hair and wearing clothes that mismatched according to fashion, but he was still short and pudgy and irregular of feature. He was also the youngest person in his school, even though he was a senior—and the only black person there, which was a factor in Virginia in 1994.

Now if love were sensible, if the sexual impulse was ever tempered by logic, you would expect that Cletus, being Cletus, would assess his situation and go off in search of someone homely. But of course he didn't. He just jingled and clanked down through the Pachinko machine of adolescence, being rejected, at first glance, by every Mary and Judy and Jenny and Veronica in Known Space, going from the ravishing to the beautiful to the pretty to the cute to the plain to the "great personality," until the irresistible force of statistics brought him finally into contact with Amy Linderbaum, who could not reject him at first glance because she was blind.

The other kids thought it was more than amusing. Besides being blind, Amy was about twice as tall as Cletus and, to be kind, equally irregular of feature. She was accompanied by a guide dog who looked remarkably like Cletus, short and black and pudgy. Everybody was polite to her because she was blind and rich, but she was a new transfer student and didn't have any actual friends.

So along came Cletus, to whom Cupid had dealt only slings and arrows, and what might otherwise have been merely an opposites-attract sort of romance became an emotional and intellectual union that, in the next century, would power a social tsunami that would irreversibly transform the human condition. But first there was the violin.

Her classmates had sensed that Amy was some kind of nerd herself, as classmates will, but they hadn't figured out what kind yet. She was pretty fast with a computer, but you could chalk that up to being blind and actually needing the damned thing. She wasn't fanatical about it, nor about science or math or history or Star Trek or student government, so what the hell kind of nerd was she? It turns out that she was a music nerd, but at the time was too painfully shy to demonstrate it.

All Cletus cared about, initially, was that she lacked those pesky Y-chromosomes and didn't recoil from him: in the Venn diagram of the human race, she was the only member of that particular set. When he found out that she was actually smart as well, having read more books than most of her classmates put together, romance began to smolder in a deep and permanent place. That was even before the violin.

Amy liked it that Cletus didn't play with her dog and was straightforward in his curiosity about what it was like to be blind. She could assess people pretty well from their voices: after one sentence, she knew that he was young, black, shy, nerdy, and not from Virginia. She could tell from his inflection that either he was unattractive or he thought he was. She

was six years older than him and white and twice his size, but otherwise they matched up pretty well, and they started keeping company in a big way.

Among the few things that Cletus did not know anything about was music. That the other kids wasted their time memorizing the words to inane top-40 songs was proof of intellectual dysfunction if not actual lunacy. Furthermore, his parents had always been fanatical devotees of opera. A universe bounded on one end by puerile mumblings about unrequited love and on the other end by foreigners screaming in agony was not a universe that Cletus desired to explore. Until Amy picked up her violin.

They talked constantly. They sat together at lunch and met between classes. When the weather was good, they sat outside before and after school and talked. Amy asked her chauffeur to please be ten or fifteen minutes late picking her up.

So after about three weeks' worth of the fullness of time, Amy asked Cletus to come over to her house for dinner. He was a little hesitant, knowing that her parents were rich, but he was also curious about that lifestyle and, face it, was smitten enough that he would have walked off a cliff if she asked him nicely. He even used some computer money to buy a nice suit, a symptom that caused his mother to grope for the Valium.

The dinner at first was awkward. Cletus was bewildered by the arsenal of silverware and all the different kinds of food that didn't look or taste like food. But he had known it was going to be a test, and he always did well on tests, even when he had to figure out the rules as he went along.

Amy had told him that her father was a self-made millionaire; his fortune had come from a set of patents in solid-state electronics. Cletus had therefore spent a Saturday at the university library, first searching patents and then reading selected texts, and he was ready at least for the father. It worked very well. Over soup, the four of them talked about computers. Over the calamari cocktail, Cletus and Mr. Linderbaum had it narrowed down to specific operating systems and partitioning schemata. With the beef Wellington, Cletus and "Call-me-Lindy" were talking quantum electrodynamics; with the salad they were on an electron cloud somewhere, and by the time the nuts were served, the two nuts at that end of the table were talking in Boolean algebra while Amy and her mother exchanged knowing sighs and hummed snatches of Gilbert and Sullivan.

By the time they retired to the music room for coffee, Lindy liked Cletus very much, and the feeling was mutual, but Cletus didn't know how much he liked Amy, really liked her, until she picked up the violin.

It wasn't a Strad—she was promised one if and when she graduated from Julliard—but it had cost more than the Lamborghini in the garage, and she was not only worth it, but equal to it. She picked it up and tuned it quietly while her mother sat down at an electronic keyboard next to the grand piano, set it to "harp," and began the simple arpeggio that a musically sophisticated person would recognize as the introduction to the violin showpiece "Méditation" from Massenet's *Thaïs*.

Cletus had turned a deaf ear to opera for all his short life, so he didn't know the backstory of transformation and transcending love behind this intermezzo, but he did know that his girlfriend had lost her sight at the age of five, and the next year—the year he was born! —was given her first violin. For thirteen years she had been using it to say what she would not say with her voice, perhaps to see what she could not see with her eyes, and on the deceptively simple romantic matrix that Massenet built to present the beautiful courtesan Thaïs gloriously reborn as the bride of Christ, Amy forgave her Godless universe for taking her sight, and praised it for what she was given in return, and she said this in a language that even Cletus could understand. He didn't cry very much, never had, but by the last high wavering note he was weeping into his hands, and he knew that if she wanted him, she could have him forever, and oddly enough, considering his age and what eventually happened, he was right.

He would learn to play the violin before he had his first doctorate, and during a lifetime of remarkable amity they would play together for ten thousand hours, but all of that would come after the big idea. The big idea—"Why aren't all blind people geniuses?"—was planted that very night, but it didn't start to sprout for another week.

Like most thirteen-year-olds, Cletus was fascinated by the human body, his own and others, but his study was more systematic than others' and, atypically, the organ that interested him most was the brain.

The brain isn't very much like a computer, although it doesn't do a bad job, considering that it's built by unskilled labor and programmed more by pure chance than anything else. One thing computers do a lot better than brains, though, is what Cletus and Lindy had been talking about over their little squids in tomato sauce: partitioning.

Think of the computer as a big meadow of green pastureland, instead of a little dark box full of number-clogged things that are expensive to replace, and that pastureland is presided over by a wise old magic shepherd who is not called a macroprogram. The shepherd stands on a hill and looks out over the pastureland, which is full of sheep and goats and cows. They aren't all in one homogeneous mass, of course, since the cows would step on the lambs and kids and the goats would make everybody nervous, leaping and butting, so there are partitions of barbed wire that keep all the species separate and happy.

This is a frenetic sort of meadow, though, with cows and goats and sheep coming in and going out all the time, moving at about 3×10^8 meters per second, and if the partitions were all of the same size it would be a disaster, because sometimes there are no sheep at all, but lots of cows, who would be jammed in there hip to hip and miserable. But the shepherd, being wise, knows ahead of time how much space to allot to the various creatures and, being magic, can move barbed wire quickly without hurting himself or the animals. So each partition winds up marking a comfortable-sized space for each use. Your computer does that too, but instead of barbed wire you see little rectangles or windows or file folders, depending on your computer's religion.

The brain has its own partitions, in a sense. Cletus knew that certain physical areas of the brain were associated with certain mental abilities, but it wasn't a simple matter of "music appreciation goes over there; long division in that corner." The brain is mushier than that. For instance, there are pretty well-defined partitions associated with linguistic functions, areas named after French and German brain people. If one of those areas is destroyed, by stroke or bullet or flung frying pan, the stricken person may lose the ability—reading or speaking or writing coherently—associated with the lost area.

That's interesting, but what is more interesting is that the lost ability sometimes comes back over time. Okay, you say, so the brain grew back—but it doesn't! You're born with all the brain cells you'll ever have. (Ask any child.) What evidently happens is that some other part of the brain has been sitting around as a kind of backup, and after a while the wiring gets rewired and hooked into that backup. The afflicted person can say his name, and then his wife's name, and then "frying pan," and before you know it he's complaining about hospital food and calling a divorce lawyer.

So on that evidence, it would appear that the brain has a shepherd like the computer-meadow has, moving partitions around, but alas, no. Most of the time when some part of the brain ceases to function, that's the end of it. There may be acres and acres of fertile ground lying fallow right next door, but nobody in charge to make use of it—at least not consistently. The fact that it sometimes did work is what made Cletus ask, "Why aren't all blind people geniuses?"

Of course there have always been great thinkers and writers and composers who were blind (and in the twentieth century, some painters to whom eyesight was irrelevant), and many of them, like Amy with her violin, felt that their talent was a compensating gift. Cletus wondered whether there might be a literal truth to that, in the micro-anatomy of the brain. It didn't happen every time, or else all blind people would be geniuses. Perhaps it happened occasionally, through a mechanism like the one that helped people recover from strokes. Perhaps it could be made to happen.

Cletus had been offered scholarships at both Harvard and MIT, but he opted for Columbia, in order to be near Amy while she was studying at Julliard. Columbia reluctantly allowed him a triple major in physiology, electrical engineering, and cognitive science, and he surprised everybody who knew him by doing only moderately well. The reason, it turned out, was that he was treating undergraduate work as a diversion at best; a necessary evil at worst. He was racing ahead of his studies in the areas that were important to him.

If he had paid more attention in trivial classes like history, like philosophy, things might have turned out differently. If he had paid attention to literature he might have read the story of Pandora.

Our own story now descends into the dark recesses of the brain. For the next ten years the main part of the story, which we will try to ignore after this paragraph, will involve Cletus doing disturbing intellectual tasks like cutting up dead brains, learning how to pronounce cholecystokinin, and sawing holes in peoples' skulls and poking around inside with live electrodes.

In the other part of the story, Amy also learned how to pronounce cholecystokinin, for the same reason that Cletus learned how to play the violin. Their love grew and mellowed, and at the age of nineteen, between his first doctorate and his M.D., Cletus paused long enough for them to be married and have a whirlwind honeymoon in Paris, where Cletus divided his time between the musky charms of his beloved and the sterile cubicles of Institute Marey, learning how squids learn things, which was by serotonin pushing adenylate cyclase to catalyze the synthesis of cyclic adenosine monophosphate in just the right place, but that's actually the main part of the story, which we have been trying to ignore, because it gets pretty gruesome.

They returned to New York, where Cletus spent eight years becoming a pretty good neurosurgeon. In his spare time he tucked away a doctorate in electrical engineering. Things began to converge.

At the age of thirteen, Cletus had noted that the brain used more cells collecting, handling, and storing visual images than it used for all the other senses combined. "Why aren't all blind people geniuses?" was just a specific case of the broader assertion, "The brain doesn't know how to make use of what it's got." His investigations over the next fourteen years were more subtle and complex than that initial question and statement, but he did wind up coming right back around to them.

Because the key to the whole thing was the visual cortex.

When a baritone saxophone player has to transpose sheet music from cello, he (few women are drawn to the instrument) merely pretends that the music is written in treble clef rather than bass, eyeballs it up an octave, and then plays without the octave key pressed down. It's so simple a child could do it, if a child wanted to play such a huge, ungainly instrument. As his eye dances along the little fenceposts of notes, his fingers automatically perform a one-to-one transformation that is the theoretical equivalent of adding and subtracting octaves, fifths, and thirds, but all of the actual mental work is done when he looks up in the top right corner of the first page and says, "Aw hell. Cello again." Cello parts aren't that interesting to saxophonists.

But the eye is the key, and the visual cortex is the lock. When blind Amy "sight-reads" for the violin, she has to stop playing and feel the Braille notes with her left hand. (Years of keeping the instrument in place while she does this has made her neck muscles so strong that she can crack a walnut between her chin and shoulder.) The visual cortex is not involved, of course; she "hears" the mute notes of a phrase with her fingertips, temporarily memorizing them, and then plays them over and over until she can add that phrase to the rest of the piece.

Like most blind musicians, Amy had a very good "ear"; it actually took her less time to memorize music by listening to it repeatedly, rather than reading, even with fairly complex pieces. (She used Braille nevertheless for serious work, so she could isolate the composer's intent from the performer's or conductor's phrasing decisions.)

She didn't really miss being able to sight-read in a conventional way. She wasn't even sure what it would be like, since she had never seen sheet music before she lost her sight, and in fact had only a vague idea of what a printed page of writing looked like.

So when her father came to her in her thirty-third year and offered to buy her the chance of a limited gift of sight, she didn't immediately jump at it. It was expensive and risky and grossly deforming: implanting miniaturized video cameras in her eye sockets and wiring them up to stimulate her dormant optic nerves. What if it made her only half blind, but also blunted her musical ability? She knew how other people read music, at least in theory, but after a quarter-century of doing without the skill, she wasn't sure that it would do much for her. It might make her tighten up.

Besides, most of her concerts were done as charities to benefit organizations for the blind or for special education. Her father argued that she would be even more effective in those venues as a recovered blind person. Still she resisted.

Cletus said he was cautiously for it. He said he had reviewed the literature and talked to the Swiss team who had successfully done the implants on dogs and primates. He said he didn't think she would be harmed by it even if the experiment failed. What he didn't say to Amy or Lindy or anybody was the grisly Frankensteinian truth: that he was himself behind the experiment; that it had nothing to do with restoring sight; that the little video cameras would never even be hooked up. They were just an excuse for surgically removing her eyeballs.

Now a normal person would have extreme feelings about popping out somebody's eyeballs for the sake of science, and even more extreme feelings on learning that it was a husband wanting to do it to his wife. Of course Cletus was far from being normal in any respect. To his way of thinking, those eyeballs were useless vestigial appendages that blocked surgical access to the optic nerves, which would be his conduits through the brain to the visual cortex. Physical conduits, through which incredibly tiny surgical instruments would be threaded. But we have promised not to investigate that part of the story in detail.

The end result was not grisly at all. Amy finally agreed to go to Geneva, and Cletus and his surgical team (all as skilled as they were unethical) put her through three twenty-hour days of painstaking but painless microsurgery, and when they took the bandages off and adjusted a thousand-dollar wig (for they'd had to go in behind as well as through the eye sockets), she actually looked more attractive than when they had started. That was partly because her actual hair had always been a disaster. And now she had glass baby-blues instead of the rather scary opalescence of her natural eyes. No Buck Rogers TV cameras peering out at the world.

He told her father that that part of the experiment hadn't worked, and the six Swiss scientists who had been hired for the purpose agreed.

"They're lying," Amy said. "They never intended to restore my sight. The sole intent of the operations was to subvert the normal functions of the visual cortex in such a way as to give me access to the un-used parts of my brain." She faced the sound of her husband's breathing, her blue eyes looking beyond him. "You have succeeded beyond your expectations."

Amy had known this as soon as the fog of drugs from the last operation had lifted. Her mind started making connections, and those connections made connections, and so on at a geometrical rate of growth. By the time they had finished putting her wig on, she had reconstructed the entire microsurgical procedure from her limited readings and conversations with Cletus. She had suggestions as to improving it, and was eager to go under and submit herself to further refinement.

As to her feelings about Cletus, in less time than it takes to read about it, she had gone from horror to hate to understanding to renewed love, and finally to an emotional condition beyond the ability of any merely natural language to express. Fortunately, the lovers did have Boolean algebra and propositional calculus at their disposal.

Cletus was one of the few people in the world she could love, or even talk to one-on-one, without condescending. His IQ was so high that its number would be meaningless. Compared to her, though, he was slow, and barely literate. It was not a situation he would tolerate for long.

The rest is history, as they say, and anthropology, as those of us left who read with our eyes must recognize every minute of every day. Cletus was the second person to have the operation done, and he had to accomplish it while on the run from medical ethics people and their policemen. There were four the next year, though, and twenty the year after that, and then two thousand and twenty thousand. Within a decade, people with purely intellectual occupations had no choice, or one choice: lose your eyes or lose your job. By then the "secondsight" operation was totally automated, totally safe.

It's still illegal in most countries, including the United States, but who is kidding whom? If your department chairman is secondsighted and you are not, do you think you'll get tenure? You can't even hold a conversation with a creature whose synapses fire six times as fast as yours, with whole encyclopedias of information instantly available. You are, like me, an intellectual throwback.

You may have a good reason for it, being a painter, an architect, a naturalist, or a trainer of guide dogs. Maybe you can't come up with the money for the operation, but that's a weak excuse, since it's trivially easy to get a loan against future earnings. Maybe there's a good physical reason for you not to lie down on that table and open your eyes for the last time.

I know Cletus and Amy through music. I was her keyboard professor once, at Julliard, though now of course I'm not smart enough to teach her anything. They come to hear me play sometimes, in this run-down bar with its band of ageing firstsight musicians. Our music must seem boring, obvious, but they do us the favor of not joining in.

Amy was an innocent bystander in this sudden evolutionary explosion. And Cletus was, arguably, blinded by love.

The rest of us have to choose which kind of blindness to endure.

Copyright © 1994 by Joe Haldeman

Barry N. Malzberg is a Hugo and Nebula nominee, the author of close to one hundred novels and four hundred stories. His column appeared in the first twenty-six issues of Galaxy's Edge, *plus twenty issues of* Jim Baen's Universe *(which Mike Resnick co-edited), and these forty-six columns have been collected into a forthcoming book,* The Bend at the End of the Road, *for which this is the Afterward.*

THE BEND AT THE END OF THE ROAD

by Barry N. Malzberg

Here are (or more appropriately, there they were) twenty essays for the twenty issues of the online "magazine" *Baen's Universe* and twenty-six from the print publication *Galaxy's Edge*, written over the decade between 2006 and 2007 and attempting to sum a long, occasionally unpleasant, less occasionally self-focused career of commentary on science fiction, the culture, the culture of science fiction and other disasters. I began writing personal essays sometime in the mid-1970s for Geis's *Science Fiction Review*, but had already done some reviewing for that publication and earlier for *Fantasy & Science Fiction*. The reviews were always awkward, not my medium and ultimately I questioned my authority and their relevance and quit.

The personal essays were, at the outset, both more and less than awkward, straining for a voice and often defaulting into complaint. (A few of those early efforts survive in the Doubleday *Engines of the Night*.) Eventually through practice, humility and some element of grace I found the proper voice and slowly improved; by the early eighties I was able to read what I had written without cringing. Very few writers of fiction are able to produce personal essays at the level of their best (or even worse) fiction; Mailer is an exception but it could be argued that he was always a polemicist; Nabokov was usually an exception but VN conformed to no ordinary standard as we know. I did get better and somewhere in the course of that improvement I found that my interest in fiction was steadily diminishing. The bibliographers can prove that I wrote it to some standard but

ever more as the polity and its politics crawled toward disaster I found that I was losing patience and faith in the form. In 1960 Phillip Roth had published a famous essay arguing that in the United States technology and its disastrous consequences had utterly overwhelmed fiction's feebler ability to invent, influence, sway a wide audience. Evident fifty-eight years ago that declaration seems now to be inarguable. There was not a novelist in town unshaken by 9/11, the catastrophic event seemed to mock the authors' necessary belief in the importance of the form itself. And now we have encountered a spectacle of power so cruel, remote, distanced and self-serving that recognizing one's helplessness seems the only logical default. Non-fiction, the personal essay, have at least the possibility of testimony, an unshielded immediacy. What does fiction possess?

In any case, a decade in the American abattoir, the abattoir which science fiction itself has become, the attempt to argue that the two dilemmas are refractory can be enormously discouraging. *Jim Baen's Universe*, after twenty issues, quit on itself and its audience, but *Galaxy's Edge*, something of a house organ for its indulgent publishers, shows no sign yet of taking that option. I therefore took it for myself. Twenty-six columns seemed like Ambrose Bierce's "Too Much" from The *Devil's Dictionary*. "Enough = Too Much." So I quit. Collected here is the Long Goodbye to the Long Result.

☼

It seemed to me—considering the Long Result in its fullest perspective —that like the political "great experiment" of our democracy, science fiction was born with its self-destruction embedded. The framers of the Constitution had ambition and ideas, but no conception (how could they?) of what technology, money, the seizure of the mediums of communication would do to the First Amendment. They had no conception that the First Amendment put "free expression" up for sale and those with the most technology, the most access, the most money would inevitably overtake any argument. Science fiction was always, both in its historical pre-Gernsback form of scientific romance and then later as a discrete post-Gernsback "form of literature to interest young boys in science" obsessed with destruction, with the cultivation of forces which would bring it ultimately to an end. It was always (as one of the later essays makes clear) a kind of literature always obsessed with the apocalyptic and the first place to which the apocalyptic impulses are drawn would be, of course, its origin. Death in life, life in death, this was a point being hammered ever more explicitly in these essays and eventually, later than I had originally anticipated but still soon enough, I was becoming sickened by the sound or transcription of my own voice, this teeny tiny Cassandra shouting its dreadful warnings and self-disgust through all of the corridors of witness. It was enough. It was not so much performance art after a while as it was performance as anti-performance. Like Wilfred Sheed's stricken critic in *Max Jamison* who wrote vicious reviews for *Partisan Review* and picked up admiring young ladies in museums, I found that it was the very *winsomeness* of this activity which was inducing a kind of self-disgust, my features becoming gradually inflated to circle the sky like Ballard's apparitions of Marilyn or then again perhaps his Drowned Giant. My graffiti of distress were being transcribed on a hundred subway walls like Paul Simon's prophets and the graffiti, the prophets had the same message: *The end is near*. It is a wearisome act. It has its components of truth and relevance but many of the prophets were ending, like Sonny Liston or Lenny Bruce, on toilet seats of possibility with a spike sunk into an arm. Enough, enough. Point taken, ladies and gents? If you cannot always leave them laughing you could, at least, leave.

✿

"Junk!" Maurice Sendak said in an interview almost fifty years ago, talking of his inspiration and mission. "I love it! I love it all!" Mickey Mouse, model airplanes, Jiggs and Maggie, cartoon dancers, fast food, dynamic obsolescence, he loved them all: junk had been institutionalized, indeed perfected in the mid-century USA in which Sendak (1928-2012) had come to maturity. Junk was the heart of the heart of the country, it was the mainspring, the gonfalon, the grand flag itself and it could be speculated that the greatest accomplishment of high art was to banish any division between itself and the boiling, steaming, fetid reservoir whose fumes signaled pronounced elevation. *The Ring Cycle* was junk: gods and goddesses and dwarves and phantom gnomish figures hammering out the gold; *Die Zauberflöte* was junk and the secret caverns of the monastery were assailed by Monostatos and mocked by Papagena; science fiction's magic flute sounded in all of its efforts great and low, and that Pied Piper drew to it First Fandom, Second Foundation, the SMOFs with all of their schemes and of course in the fullness of time science fiction became the man who ate the world: first by force in Hiroshima and eventually through the creepy extrusion of magic and madness into every aspect of the common life until it was impossible to disentangle the two. "My drug-crazed visions of the 60s, my made-up universe," Phil Dick said to me at midnight in 1974 on the telephone, our only conversation, "has become something which has taken over every aspect of our lives. Do you know how this makes me feel? Does anybody?"

✿

Mailer's "Superman Comes to Supermart," "A Thousand Words a Minute," and "In the Red Light" overwhelmed me in the early 1960s. Those three *Esquire* essays seemed to demonstrate exactly the route I wanted to take, to show the country to itself, to show how the heaving, brutish underlay, the damaged history, the blood guilt and ruin which Faulkner announced were barely suppressed by the glitter and trash, that trashy glitter then of entertainment, the hum of religion (Stanley Elkin's "Great Wow") were laid unevenly and ineptly over those surfaces as a form of denial which itself in splendid mockery and assumption simply became another aspect of the junk, so interwoven with Marilyn and Elvis and Marvel Comics that all of it was a kind of prayer. Science fiction too was a prayer, a ritual of technology explained as curse or divinity, make that divinity's curse then and I tried to work that angle in my own prose. Essays would have to wait, no one was interested in my opinion, and it was all too close in the 60s to that of Mailer, expressed far less eloquently. Science fiction was the place to go. Quality lit wanted no part of me, *Esquire* was not likely to take my essays if

Mailer was on the job. "I used to read a lot of this stuff when I was a kid," I decided. "Maybe I can make a go of this." I certainly had nowhere else to go. I have written of this dialogue and decision many times in many venues, making the point over and again. Perhaps I was trying to convince myself. Maybe I was retrospectively assigning a kind of seriousness and sense of mission which did not exist at the time. A certain kind of adolescent was not likely to say, at least to himself, "I want to get laid." He had to frame that for the cleaned-up version of himself he needed for reasons barely to be expressed as, "I want to find true love." As if there was always such a schism. Junk knew better. Junk knew how to leap the chasm. Junk could move mountains.

☼

But it seemed necessary in any case to force the issue, put the issue, perhaps if I could hit it hard and often enough in the same place I could get through and those were the essays from the beginning, from the first halting efforts in *Science Fiction Review* to those less halting efforts as I acquired or at least was able to simulate some kind of voice. Throughout I was haunted by Vidal's view of Dos Passos' last novel, *Mid-Century*, "an old man confusing his own deterioration for a deterioration of the world." It is not uncommon, but I acted as if I was alert to it and would be able to manage its disastrous deterioration. Retrospectively, I am not so sure. It might have happened to me after all. To be alert may be only another species of delusion. Then too, there was Budrys' terrible self-indulgence and mumbling of a Concealed History of the World (which he would necessarily keep to himself). "I am living a secret life," the critic would imply. "The full knowledge of which would leave you incapable."

☼

So in the end you do what you can. As Hemingway wrote ending *Death in the Afternoon*, you do your work and not too damned late and then you walk away from it. I had serious purposes and so did science fiction, but in the end our souls had reached the same conclusion: it was the junk from and to which we were drawn and it would be the junk, not

the aspiration, which would save the world. If the world could be saved. If our lives could be anointed. If the words of the prophets were truly our own and rendered in enormous letters on the subway walls. Or perhaps became skywriting in the sky.

Copyright © 2018 by Barry N. Malzberg

Jody Lynn Nye is the author of forty novels and more than one hundred stories, and has at various times collaborated with Anne McCaffrey and Robert Asprin. Her husband, Bill Fawcett, is a prolific author, editor and packager, and is also active in the gaming field.

BOOK RECOMMENDATIONS

by Jody Lynn Nye and Bill Fawcett

Though Hell Should Bar the Way
by David Drake
Baen Books
April 2018
ISBN-13: 978-1481483131

David Drake's RCN books featuring Captain Leary have been a top-selling series for years. The Republic of Cinnabar Navy universe is one of star empires and full of shifting alliances and cutthroat espionage. David Drake has commented that it is modelled on the period between the two Punic Wars between Rome and Carthage. Interestingly, both heroes serve in the navy of a mercantile oligarchy similar to Carthage. Which is not as dark as it sounds since his characters are unaware of their historical precedent. It is not beyond Mr. Drake to find a way for the merchant princes to win this time.

What makes *Though Hell Should Bar the Way* noteworthy is not only the writing and great story, but—and this is something rare in our era of twelve-book trilogies and never-ending series—it's the first book of a new series set in the same RCN universe. It introduces a new character, Roy Olfetrie, who becomes a member of Leary's crew and then things happen to him, lots of things, mostly very unpleasant.

The book focuses on this new character. Olfetrie was a cadet but had to quit when his father is discovered to have been stealing massively from navy contracts. When the book opens, Olfetrie is struggling at an unskilled job at a shipyard. He is provoked into decking the obnoxious son-in-law of the owner. Fortunately he does this in front of several of Leary's crew, who are impressed by his guts, and soon finds himself as the captain's third officer on a ship carrying a diplomatic delegation to a minor star empire.

Roy finds himself approached to become a spy. He is shanghaied, then enslaved, but through nerve and a bit of financial cunning soon changes not only his situation, but an entire planet's future. Along with Drake's typically great action, gritty realism, and well-drawn characterizations, you also see more of a fascinating universe from a new perspective.

Whether you have read the rest of the RCN novels or not, this book is a quick, fun read. If you are new to the series, this is a great place to start, knowing that there are half a dozen more good books set in the same worlds already available.

Once it starts rolling, you cannot put *Though Hell Should Bar the Way* down. In other words, it's exactly what we expect from any military science-fiction novel by such a master of the field. Highly recommended for hard SF readers, action junkies, military SF fans and those who enjoy a multi-world jaunt fraught with betrayal, heroism, and desperation.

✧

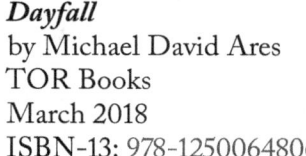

✧

Dayfall
by Michael David Ares
TOR Books
March 2018
ISBN-13: 978-1250064806

If you are a fan of Dashiell Hammett's Sam Spade, this is a book you will really enjoy. A police detective is on the hunt for a serial killer across a dystopian New York City that is facing its first real sunny day in forty years. The concept was obviously inspired by the exact opposite situation in the classic Isaac Asimov story *Nightfall*. But here, due to an atomic war in Asia complicated by massive global warming, the sun has been obscured for decades over much of the Northern Hemisphere. A somewhat shrunken Atlantic Ocean has flooded half the borough, and Manhattan is in the middle of political and social unrest with a serial killer enhancing the near panic any change, even a return to sunlight days, often brings. The mystery works, the main character is very human while still being as hard-edged and determined as any pulp detective. If you will enjoy an urban murder mystery, cutthroat politicians, and the seamy underside of a dystopian New York City, don't miss *Dayfall*.

Pacifica
by Kristen Simmons
TOR Teen
March 2018
ISBN-13: 978-0765336637

This dystopian story is one of the best and most colorfully drawn dark futures out there. More importantly, the book does not preach but simply uses the setting as the basis of a really well told action story with suitable doses of both romance and coming-of-age troubles and angst.

With a dramatic increase in carbon dioxide the oceans have risen not a few feet, but hundreds. All that remains of California are mountain-top islands. Humanity has been driven up the sides of the Rocky Mountains. Thousands huddle at the base of the last real city, mostly facing starvation and oppression on the shores of an enlarged Pacific Ocean wracked by massive storms.

Ron Torres is the sheltered son of the charismatic president of this last city. He and the elite live opulent lives. Ron and a friend, who is the token underprivileged student at his private school, decide to sneak out and see one of the almost daily riots. Neither youth is ready for either the sheer hopelessness of the poorer areas or the dangers of the reality of desperate people rioting and police putting them down using extreme force. The friends are separated, and Ron finds himself imprisoned by mistake, then fleeing with a fellow prisoner, the street—and ocean-savvy Marin. It soon turns out that Marin was the daughter and is now sister of a pirate leader whose base is an island that is really a gigantic floating aggregation of plastics and waste. The young protagonists fall into a series of adventures, betrayals, romance, and sea-faring saga all involving with a plot to relocate the poor to an island paradise that does not really exist.

One of the strengths of this book is the excellent portrayal of the emotions of the characters. The resentment of the oppressed and their desperation, the courage of the young heroes, and the greed and arrogance of those who just want to get rid of the annoying masses are an integral part of this very dark dystopia. This is a very readable cultural and high-seas adventure.

☼

Chasing Shadows: Visions of Our Coming Transparent World
Edited by David Brin and Stephen W. Potts
TOR Books
January 2017
ISBN-13: 978-0765382580

The subtitle of this anthology is "Visions of Our Coming Transparent World." All the stories relate to communication and human interaction as modified by technology, and privacy. There are over thirty stories by many of the top writers in SF. Each is categorized under such sections as Big Brother, Surveillance, No Place to Hide, and Lies and Private Lies. Some of the stories and short essays included were written from as far back as the 60s, though more than half of the stories are new.

In a way, it was hard to review this anthology. The usual approach doesn't apply. At the risk of frightening off readers, I have to say that this is a collection of stories that has something important to say about an issue that is vitally important to your world today,

not something you can very often say about a SF anthology. Each story in each topic shows how SF authors have been concerned about the questions of privacy, control of one's own data or even oneself, and the consequences of technology that will affect the coming decades. More importantly this rather large anthology is brimming with excellent, well-written and sometimes frightening or uncomfortable stories.

Normally you pick out a few outstanding entries that justify the collection. But who to pick from this one is a problem. There are classics such as William Gibson's "The Road to Oceana," emotionally evocative classics such as Damon Knight's "I See You," and Robert Silverberg's "The Invisible Man." There are stories with an open warning such as Jack McDevitt's "Your Lying Eyes" or David Brin's "Insistence of Vision." (You will never look at Apple glasses the same way again after reading David's story.) The original stories in the volume are of equal quality and impact. There is no way to avoid one cliché phrase when describing these stories: *thought provoking*. Read this just after signing off from Google, or looking up someone on Facebook.

☼

Meet Me in the Strange
by Leander Watts
Meerkat Press
March 2018
ISBN-13: 978-1946154156

Meet Me in the Strange is a young adult book that takes place in an alternate Venice in 1970, the year after the Apollonauts, as Davi, the first-person narrator calls them, landed on the moon. It opens in the midst of a rock concert starring the glamorous Django Conn, an analogue of David Bowie, with all his marvelous trappings and cosmic mystery. The vibe of Django's music lifts the teenage Davi into what he feels is another level of consciousness. To him, it is something wider, higher, and more important than humans, like most of the other fans in the crowd are normally capable of experiencing or comprehending. Davi notices a girl dancing by herself—a plain girl with wild black hair and glasses. She, too, seems to have become caught up in the mystic vibe. Davi tries to meet her but she disappears.

Davi lives in the Angelus, a sprawling, century-old grand hotel that has been owned by his family for generations. He and his sister occupy suites on the same floor but seldom interact with one another or their widowed father. Both of them have their own interests: Sabina dabbles in New Age mysteries like séances and spells, with dubious characters like the sinister Carlos. Davi lives for music, such as Django's and other bands with evocative names that are chords of 1970's acts in our Earth. He spots the mystery girl emerging from Sabina's door and follows her out into the city.

They finally meet. She had noticed him at the concert too. Her name is Anna Z., and she is fantastic and endlessly talkative. She explains to Davi that the vibe they both experienced was a function of the Alien Drift, which allows certain humans to tap into the infinite. Both she and Davi have felt alone but now they have one another. It's not all smooth or easy for them. Anna has an older brother, Lukas, who is possessive and dangerous. He feels that he owns her, that she is his creation like Frankenstein's monster, a comparison that comes up several times in the narrative. She has run away from him before, but never with someone who understood her and would help her, someone who understood the beauty and mystery of the coming contact with alien intelligence. Lukas knows Davi is hiding her, and threatens to kill him if Davi doesn't bring Anna back to him.

They learn that Django is leaving the concert circuit. His last performance with his band will be at a venue a hundred miles from Davi's city. The two teens know they have to be there, so they must sneak out of the city under Lukas's nose.

The book is written in a poetic, cadenced style that is almost music in itself. It lays a glamour over what might be a prosaic story of a boy and a girl meeting in an old, fairly ordinary city. The imagery is beautiful and evocative, from the glister boys and glam girls in the concert audience to the electrum light flowing over the city that only Anna and Davi understand. Sprinkled throughout are lyrics from some of Django's songs, and the reader can dig meaning from them as the teen protagonists do. Watts understands the need that young people have to belong to something. Rock music and Django himself provide Davi and Anna with a common language that is a launch pad to a higher experience that bonds them and gives them purpose. Though the teens are passionately attracted to one another, their relationship is a fairly pure one. *Meet Me at the Strange* is recommended for young adults and fans of the glamour rock scene.

✿

Writers of the Future, Volume 34
Edited by David Farland
Galaxy Press
April 2018
ISBN-13: 978-1619865754

There are a number of good reasons why you should read this anthology. One is that the selection of stories is excellent. There are no weak stories. *Writers of the Future* gets thousands of entries from all over the world each year and collects only the best. Another is that in the past volumes you would have discovered early winning new talent such as Eric Flint, Brandon Sanderson, K. D. Wentworth and more now familiar names. There is also a number of insightful essays, including some good advice for new writers that might have been the last thing Jerry Pournelle wrote. The stories are all matched with high quality color art by up-and-coming new artists from the Illustrators of the Future contest.

Publishers Weekly just reviewed this anthology, and agreed about the high quality of the stories. In a starred review, they pointed out two as outstanding. One by a contest judge, Jody Lynn Nye (the co-author of this column), "Illusion," tells how a very sneaky illusionist saves his kingdom from invasion. The other is "Odd and Ugly" by Vida Cruz. This story, based on a Philippine myth, is told from the point of view of a gnarled forest creature. The strength of the emotions, familiar yet exotic color, and ending of the story will surprise and delight.

Other outstanding stories include the tale of a most unusual android, "A Smokeless and Scorching Fire" by Eric Cairns, a vibrantly told and rousing story of rebellion and magic by Jeremy TeGrotenhuis, "The Minarets of An-Zarat." You will assuredly be a little disturbed by the vividly written "Mara's Shadow," a tale of how a DNA-changing parasite almost destroys humanity.

To get a preview of future bestsellers and to just enjoy over four hundred and fifty pages of well-written and beautifully illustrated stories and novellas, read *Writers of the Future, Volume 34*. And yes, seeing the quality of the writing from these new, young authors does keep us oldies looking over our shoulders.

Mission to Methoné
by Les Johnson
Baen Books
February 2018

ISBN-13: 978-1481483056

Dr. Chris Holt is a scientist whose job is to oversee spacegoing drones that fly past asteroids to analyze them for mining. One of his tiny craft comes upon a near-Earth object (NEO) that is of unusually regular shape, a perfect oval. On closer observation, he realizes that it can't possibly be natural. In fact, it is not. (Thanks to the prologue, the reader will already know its origin: an artifact from an ancient civilization that once had an outpost on the moon and was the victim of an interstellar war.) He and a multi-national crew of astronauts (American, Finnish, Japanese, and Chinese) seek to learn its secrets.

During their initial encounter, the object allows them to enter, and communicates with them. It's badly damaged and incapable of defending itself against yet another spacegoing Earth nation, the Caliphate, which has sent a missile to destroy it. Before the missile strikes, the object sends schematics and a message for Holt to bring to its counterpart a fellow Guardian orbiting Saturn in a device that human astronomers have dubbed Methoné, seeing it as an unusually regularly shaped moon.

Johnson weaves science along with human nature and politics into a compelling adventure. Holt, his fellow scientists, military advisors, politicians, and ordinary people all have a stake in discovering the truth about Methoné, but their agendas may not be the same, nor can they be certain as to the motive that the Guardians have toward humankind.

Mission to Methoné is a good, compelling read that will educate readers not only on science involved in astrophysics and space travel and the way multi-billion-dollar space projects come to fruition, but in exploring human nature and humanity's place in the universe. Johnson has a talent for providing lots of scientific fact in a way that informs and does not confuse the reader who doesn't have his training as a NASA physicist. Recommended for readers who enjoy hard science fiction but with a speculative eye toward what other intelligent life might be out there in space.

✧

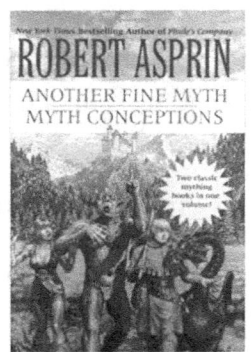

Another Fine Myth
by Robert Asprin
Starblaze Donning; Ace SF; Meish Merlin Books;
Event Horizon Press (ebooks)
April 2002
ISBN-13: 978-0441009312

First came the era of grand, sweeping fantasy epics and life-or-death quests undertaken by true-hearted heroes who must not fail lest that failure result in the destruction of an entire world or a whole population. To some, these were fascinating tomes of legitimate literary value. To others, they were pretentious and tedious, and maybe just a little too serious for reading in between final exams or equally tedious work assignments. Into the breach leaped one Robert Lynn Asprin, a natural storyteller and raconteur with a wicked sense of humor and a taste for really awful puns who enjoyed nothing more than sticking his literary thumb into the eye of droning jeremiads.

Another Fine Myth is the first of a (so far) twenty-book series known as the Myth Adventures. Skeeve, an apprentice magician, is caught out by his master Garkin when he accidentally reveals that he plans to use his newfound skills at magik (spelling is consistent throughout the series; get used to it) to break into houses and rob them. Sorrowfully, Garkin tells Skeeve that magik is deeply important and should not be taken lightly. To impress his not-terribly-impressed apprentice, he begins to summon up a demon. A figure begins to take shape in the pentagram, a hideous creature with green scales, long, sharp teeth, bat-wing ears, and yellow eyes. At that moment, Garkin is shot dead through the window of the cottage by an imp assassin with a crossbow and heat-seeking, armor-piercing quarrels. Skeeve is left alone in the room with the body of his master and the demon in the pentagram—which Skeeve notices is not completely sealed.

It turns out that the demon in question ("demon" being short for "dimensional traveler") is an old buddy of Garkin's named Aahz. The two of them used to take turns scaring one another's apprentices. But as a practical joke, just before he made Aahz appear, Garkin took away his old buddy's magikal powers. The two of them, an untrained apprentice and a master magician with no magik, realize they have to team up to stay alive. Aahz takes Skeeve on as his own apprentice. The two of them set out to try to restore Aahz's magik and neutralize the threat that killed Garkin. Along the way, they meet up with numerous old friends and acquaintances of Aahz's including a fantastically sexy assassin, acquire the world's cutest dragon, con a would-be demon hunter out of his sword, his war unicorn and most of his cash, and the rest is humorous fantasy epic history. Aahz turns out to not be as grouchy as he seemed, and Skeeve discovers he is a lot more honest than he would have believed at the beginning. At the head of each chapter featuring Skeeve is a quote from a notable personage, such as "One must deal openly and fairly with one's forces if maximum effectiveness is to be achieved."—D. Vader. Twenty-eighteen marks the fortieth anniversary of the first publication of *Another Fine Myth* by Donning-Starblaze. The original edition was illustrated by Kelly Freas, and the second (and probably more familiar) by Phil Foglio. Recommended for anyone from young adult on up who needs a good laugh.

Copyright © 2018 by Jody Lynn Nye and Bill Fawcett

Gregory Benford is a Nebula winner and a for-mer Worldcon Guest of Honor. He is the author of more than thirty novels, six books of non-fic-tion, and has edited ten anthologies.

A SCIENTIST'S NOTEBOOK

by Gregory Benford

ANTAGONISTIC PLEIOTROPY: AGING COMES FROM EVOLUTION

Aging isn't a bug or a feature of life; it's an in-evitable side effect.

Exactly why evolution favors aging is con-troversial, but plainly it does; all creatures die. It's not a curse from God or imposed by limited natu-ral resources. Aging arises from favoring short-term benefits, mostly early reproduction, over long-term survival, when reproduction has stopped.

Thermodynamics doesn't demand senescence, though early thinkers imagined it did. Similarly, ge-neric damage or "wear and tear" theories can't explain why biologically similar organisms show dramati-cally different lifespans. Most organisms maintain themselves efficiently until adulthood and then, after they can't reproduce anymore, succumb to age-re-lated damage. Some die swiftly, like flies, and others like we humans can live far beyond reproduction.

Peter Medawar introduced the idea that ageing was a matter of communication failure between gen-erations. Older organisms have no way to pass on genes that helped them survive, if they've stopped having offspring.

Nature is a highly competitive place, and almost all animals in nature die before they attain old age. Those who do can't pass newly arising, long-lived genes, so old age is naturally selected against. Ge-netically, detrimental mutations, these would not be efficiently weeded out by natural selection. Hence they would "accumulate" and, perhaps, cause all the decline and damage.

It turns out that the genes that cause ageing are not random mutations. Rather, they form tight-knit families that have been around as long as worms and fruit flies. They survive for good reasons.

In 1957 George Williams proposed his own the-ory, called antagonistic pleiotropy. If a gene has two or more effects, with one beneficial and another det-rimental, the bad one exacts a cost later on. If evolu-tion is a race to have the most offspring the fastest, then enhanced early fertility could be selected even if it came with a price tag that included decline and death later on. Because ageing was a side effect of necessary functions, Williams considered any altera-tion of the ageing process to be impossible. Antag-onistic pleiotropy is a prevailing theory today, but Williams was wrong: we can offset such effects.

Wear and tear can be countered. Wounds heal, dead cells get replaced, claws regrow. Some species are better at maintenance and repair. Medawar did not agree with Williams that there were fundamen-tal limitations on lifespan. He pointed out organ-isms like sea turtles live great spans, over a century, showing that aging is not a fundamental limitation. It arises from failure to repair, which can be ad-dressed without implying unacceptable side effects. Some species, like us, have better maintenance and repair mechanisms. These can be enhanced.

Some pursued this by deliberately aging animals, like UC Irvine's Michael Rose. Rose simply didn't let fruit fly eggs hatch until half each fly generation had died. This eliminated some genes that promoted ear-ly reproduction but had bad effects later. Over seven hundred generations later, his fruit flies live over four times longer than the control flies. These Methuse-lahs are more robust than ordinary flies and repro-duce more, not less, as some biologists predicted.

Delaying reproduction gradually extends the av-erage lifetime. One side realization: University grad-uates mate and have children later in life than oth-ers. They are then slowly selecting for longevity in those better educated. Education roughly correlates with intelligence. Eventually, longevity will correlate more and more with intelligence.

I bought these Methuselah flies in 2006 and formed a company, Genescient, to explore their ge-netics. We discovered hundreds of longevity genes shared by both flies and humans. Up-regulating the functioning of those repair genes has led to positive effects in human trials.

Genescient used the genes that conferred these benefits, which also appear in humans. Years of studying how this happens has now yielded a drug that counters Alzheimer's disease. The company has gotten a patent and permission to sell this. I believe the net effect is to up-regulate repair. A human trial shows positive effects. Expect more such effects in future.

So though aging is inevitable and emerges from antagonistic pleiotropy, it can be attacked. Recent developments point toward possibly major progress.

For example, a decade ago, the Japanese biologist Shinya Yamanaka found four crucial genes that reset the clock of the fertilized egg. However old parents are, their progeny are free of all marks of age; babies begin anew. This is a crucial feature of all creatures. By using his four genes, Yamanaka changed adult tissue cells into cells much like embryonic stem cells. Applying this reprogramming to adult tissue is tricky, but it beckons as a method of rejuvenating our own bodies.

So though evolution discards us as messengers to our descendants, once we stop reproducing, not all is lost. In the game of life, intelligence bats last.

Copyright © 2018 by Gregory Benford

Robert J. Sawyer is the Hugo, Nebula, Campbell Memorial, Heinlein, Hal Clement, Skylark, Aurora, and Seiun Award-winning author of twenty-three bestselling science-fiction novels, including the trilogy of Hominids, Humans, *and* Hybrids, *which won Canada's Aurora Award for the Best Work of the Decade. Rob holds two honorary doctorates and is a Member of the Order of Canada, the highest civilian honor bestowed by the Canadian government. Find him online at sfwriter.com.*

DECOHERENCE

by Robert J. Sawyer

APPROPRIATION

One of my proudest moments came at the Toronto Public Library's Book Lover's Ball in 2007. The conclusion of that fundraising banquet was the presentation to me of the annual Toronto Public Library Celebrates Reading Award—and yes, I was happy to receive this honor, but my pride was not in the trophy but rather in the zinger I was able to deliver as it was about to be handed to me.

See, it was incumbent upon the previous year's winner to present the award to the new recipient, and the year before the winner had been none other than Margaret Atwood. In bestowing the award, Margaret concluded her comments with "…and I'd just like to say how pleased I am to be seeing this go to a science-fiction writer."

To which I immediately responded, "And Margaret, I'd just like to say how pleased I am to be getting this *from* a science-fiction writer." My quip brought the house down.

Then and now, Atwood was most famous for her 1985 novel *The Handmaid's Tale*, the story of a future America in which a far-right Christian group has seized power and is subjugating women. But Margaret had always denied publicly that her book was science fiction. In fact, there was an old TV interview between her and her publisher, the late great Jack McClelland, on this very point, with them both agreeing at once that referring to her then-forthcoming novel as SF would have been marketing suicide.

Fair enough. Michael Crichton's publisher had earlier made the same decision, and that had propelled him out of the SF sales ghetto onto bestsellers' lists worldwide; I don't begrudge anyone their marketing strategies in this parlous business of books. (Still, the world knew better: *The Handmaid's Tale* was nominated for the Science Fiction Writers of America's Nebula Award and won the first-ever Arthur C. Clarke Award from the British Science Fiction Association.)

But soon Atwood went beyond merely denying her work was science fiction to dumping on the science-fiction genre as a whole—and that I could not abide. On the BBC One TV program *Breakfast News*, Margaret dismissed SF as merely "talking squids in outer space." (One of these days, I really must ask Ted Chiang if the talking squids *from* outer space that feature in his 1998 Nebula Award-winning novella "Story of Your Life," later filmed as *Arrival*, were a gentle rebuke of Ms. Atwood.)

I knew that Margaret knew better. She'd been a customer at Toronto's Bakka Books, now the world's oldest extant science-fiction specialty bookstore, when I was a clerk there in 1982; I regret not having saved the carbon paper with her autograph from the credit-card slip she signed when I sold her a book.

It's a truism that Americans tend to be ahead of Canadians on technological advancements while Canadians tend to be ahead of Americans on sociological ones. Recently, American literary circles have become inflamed over the notion of appropriation of voice—the question of whether a writer can do justice to cultures, ethnicities, or genders other than their own and, even if they can, whether it is fair for a writer from a dominant group to profit by publishing stories that perhaps more rightly should be told by the marginalized people who have actually experienced them.

At the 1989 Annual General Meeting of The Writers' Union of Canada—of which Ms. Atwood was a founding member (and I now a disaffected apostate)—Lenore Keeshig-Tobias, a writer and member of the Chippewas of Nawash Unceded First Nation, pointed out (to quote her subsequent op-ed in *The Globe and Mail*), "Stories, you see, are not just entertainment. Stories are power. They reflect the deepest, the most intimate perceptions, relationships and attitudes of a people. Stories show how a people, a culture, thinks. Such wonderful offerings are seldom reproduced by outsiders."

I'd never for a moment equate a literary culture, such as the science-fiction field (as founded by Mary Shelley a mere two hundred years ago, nurtured by H.G. Wells, and developed by those of us who have labored under the name "science fiction" since Hugo Gernsback coined that phrase in 1926) with the deep spiritual well that is a real human culture; I honor and respect diversity and multiculturalism too much for that. Still, there *is* a parallel to be made here: writers such as Atwood and Crichton and Kazuo Ishiguro and Kurt Vonnegut, who take from science fiction without acknowledging it, *are* appropriating a voice, a mode of thinking, and a style of expression (and, yes, I'll stack the best of the SF field's prose stylists against anyone from outside it).

Not only is doing that dishonest, but it has contributed mightily to the prejudice against SF that infects university hiring committees, arts councils, newspaper book-review sections, and the reading public at large, because it suggests to benighted souls that SF *can't* be literature. Or, as Kingsley Amis famously observed:

"SF's no good!" they holler 'til we're deaf
"But this is good!"
"Well then, it's not SF!"

It's also debilitating to SF when mainstream writers present warmed-over ideas taken from our genre as if they were their own invention. In Margaret Atwood's 2003 science-fiction novel *Oryx and Crake*, she borrows, and waters down, the "Chicken Little" notion from *The Space Merchants* by Frederik Pohl and C.M. Kornbluth, published forty-one years earlier, while presenting it as an innovative idea. Credit where credit is due!

Still, I had a breakthrough just last night when, over dinner, a friend said that she'd come to realize, through listening to me, that she actually likes science fiction—she just hadn't known *what* science fiction is. I told my friend I was very pleased—while thinking, "Thanks for nothing, Margaret Atwood."

Of course, Margaret and I are both Canadians, and we Canucks are famous for going around telling Americans what things they think are theirs are actually ours ("Basketball? A Canadian invented that!" "Raymond Burr? Canadian!"). But really, all of us who love science fiction need to adopt a similar strategy: if you see SF, *say* SF.

Copyright © 2018 by Robert J. Sawyer

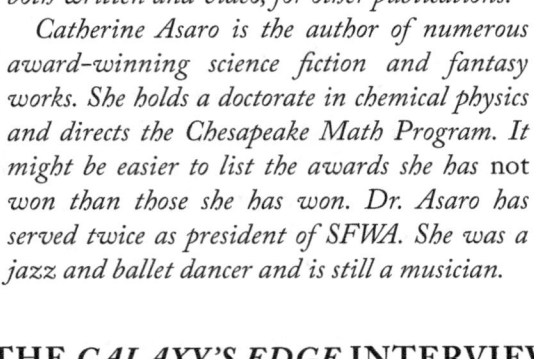

Joy Ward is the author of one novel. She has several stories in print, in magazines and in anthologies, and has also conducted interviews, both written and video, for other publications.

Catherine Asaro is the author of numerous award-winning science fiction and fantasy works. She holds a doctorate in chemical physics and directs the Chesapeake Math Program. It might be easier to list the awards she has not won than those she has won. Dr. Asaro has served twice as president of SFWA. She was a jazz and ballet dancer and is still a musician.

THE *GALAXY'S EDGE* INTERVIEW

Joy Ward Interviews Catherine Asaro

Joy Ward: How did you get into writing science fiction?

Catherine Asaro: When I was a kid I used to make up stories. When I was really little they were about this sort of nebulous girl who was, when I was five, she was seven, and she'd go out and save the galaxy. I didn't know I was making up stories. I thought everybody did this. I would daydream.

Then I found science fiction. Space Cat was my first set of science fiction stories. I thought this was just cool, the idea of these kids going to the moon or this cat going with this astronaut to Venus and so I started reading science fiction voluminously.

I had a brother and a father who liked it so I'd steal their books—until my father found out I was stealing books with sex scenes. Then the books all disappeared. I didn't quite get them (the sex scenes). But I just loved the science fiction, and I always made up stories. I didn't know at first why many of the books didn't quite work for me. All I knew is that when I made up stories, the central character, and I didn't think about it for many years, but she was always a girl.

Around the time I was twelve or thirteen, I started making the connection. There are no girls that play substantial roles in these books. Even when they are, they're usually there to support a male character. It wasn't that I was making some great statement by stopping reading. I just kind of lost interest. I couldn't find books that spoke to me since I was becoming a teenager and I'd figured out that boys were different than girls, in very interesting ways, ways I wanted to explore more. The books didn't really speak to me, but I did keep making up the stories in my mind. I never made the connection with that and the fact that I was making up stories about very strong female characters who ruled civilizations and went out on adventures until the boy next door—actually it was the boy across the street. We were down in the park, you know, doing that sort of flirting thing that teenagers—thirteen, fourteen year olds—do. He said, "Tell me your stories." So I started telling some and he listened, and he goes, "Well that's cool." Then he said, "But how come all the main characters are girls?" Until that point I hadn't made the connection. Then I thought, well should I make main characters the guys? I thought, well sure yeah, but then I thought I don't have to do it; it's my stories. But I did. I mean it wasn't on purpose. The guys are in there, the romantic interest. So the cats got replaced with handsome young pirates.

JW: When did you start writing down the stories?

CA: I tried once when I was about maybe nine. I drew pictures of the characters. Then I tried to write a story and I realized that the main character, it was a girl, she's going to rescue the male, the handsome pilot. He'd been captured and was in the enemy military installation. She went to this installation to help him escape. I got her into the military installation and I got stuck. I finally realized I had no idea what went on in military installations. I could have just gone to my parents and asked how do you do research? But I didn't. I just quit writing.

It was strange. I knew I had to do research and I didn't know how to do it. I just kept making the stories up in my head. They matured over time. Then in college I started writing. My last semester at college I only had to take one class. I had all this free time. I wrote a book by longhand on yellow legal paper. There's two things. I wanted to revise it extensively. I knew it needed it. I also didn't know at the time I'm dyslexic. I just knew that I was having trouble writing it in longhand. I thought two things. To revise this the way I want is going to take a huge amount of time because you have to rewrite it and I said it's hard for me to write. The other thing was the way it took over my life. I knew if I went to grad school I had to concentrate. So I didn't write for about another three years.

Then in grad school when I was working on my doctorate I thought, I need something. I can't look at equations anymore. I need a break. I started writing what, at the time, was the *Last Hawk*. I wrote some other stuff first and then I wrote *The Last Hawk*. And it took over again. I mean, I didn't know at the time I was the classic writer who can't think of anything else but writing. I just knew it took over and it delayed my thesis by at least six months, maybe a year.

But I finally knew how to do research. I finally knew what I wanted and what I had to do to get it and how to write the stories. I don't think I've ever stopped since then. Things got in the way, like I was a professor for a while.

JW: You've got two really distinct worlds you're working in. What is it that you get from the science fiction world that you don't really get from the mathematical and physics world?

CA: I love math, I couldn't imagine not doing it. I love writing. They are very different. Often the question I get is, what's the difference between ballet—I was a ballet dancer for many years. But I trained for years. I performed and I established dance companies when I was in graduate school. So that's often the question I get and, to me, the math and dance are not that different. Just like there's a connection between music and math.

Now that more girls are going into math and more boys are going into ballet, they're finding out there's a very strong connection between being good at ballet and being good at math. They both involve understanding spatial perception. All the music-math connection is there. But dancers are incorporating it into their body. It's not surprising that dancers and math go together. Writing for me is different. It accesses a different part of my brain.

I usually know when I've done enough because I write it and then I go back and I go through the whole thing again revising. I write really fast the first time through and it's a mess. Then I go back and it's like cleaning it up. Every time I go through I clean it up, and I finally reach a point where I'm not stopping and rewriting. But I'm never done. I could keep doing this for another year. There comes a point when you have to say, all right. I never feel like the prose is as beautiful as I want to make it. I know if I spent more time and effort I could make it even better but you have to at some point.

For each story there's usually a scene that is close to my heart. Often there's more than one scene. I choreograph them in my head and I listen to music. There'll be certain scenes, like in *Undercity* there's a scene where this person is supposed to bring members of the Undercity to this shadowy, mysterious place to be tested for these special abilities. That scene meant a lot to me when I wrote it. I imagined it in my head and choreographed it to music. I had music and I choreographed the whole thing over and over and I'd listen to it. When I finally got to writing it, I had to write it and rewrite it to get it right. When I finished that I was glad. I said, "It's done. I'm happy and this is pretty good." Then of course it got edited and edited and edited because it was too long. I put everything I imagined into it and I actually weakened it because it was too long.

It had a lot of revising but I think for me the high point was actually imagining it in my head. It does something. All my life I would imagine these things in my head to music, long before I was writing. It did something for me, to the point where my personality, my psychology, is connected with my ability to turn on music and imagine stories. I'm not as satisfied, happy with my life if I don't do that at least a little bit.

The times when I haven't been creating, when I've had a nine-to-five job, like being a professor and going home, doing homework—there's not a whole lot of time when you're a professor to do anything else— were very frustrating for me. I was not happy with that world. I sometimes almost regret that because, had I been happy to do that, I could have done a lot.

I could have become well-known in my field and I could have pushed harder and been a better role model for young women who want to go in sciences and math and all this stuff. I sometimes regret that I didn't enjoy living that way, but I didn't. I love writing and I love running this math program because I'm in charge of it.

I just would like to see more young women go into math and science. I'm trying to think of ways to get girls interested in math because right around the middle school level they start dropping out in huge numbers. I understand better now that I'm so directly involved with it. There's a very different dynamic between boys that age and girls that age. The girls just seem to grow up a little faster. When you put those groups together they're charming. All of them are charming but they're interacting in very different ways so, the boys are still boisterous, youthful and, you know, most of them are very young. The girls just sit there very quietly kind of looking around. Then they don't come back because they don't feel comfortable. So I'm trying to figure out ways to make the girls more comfortable. One thing I'm trying is dividing the classes up. Give the girls their own class. Then they come out of their shell more. I'm just trying to think of ways to involve them.

I know a lot of women write to me about reading the books and I did not set out to write strong female characters because this will have such-and-such affect. I just wrote them. But they apparently speak a lot to a lot of women. The books are not YA. They're read a lot by teenagers including some that I told my daughter she couldn't read but she did anyway.

I was the guest of honor at a convention. I remember a young woman, I saw her walking by and looking like she wanted to say something and then she went away. Later she came back and she had a card for me. She said, "I hope I'm not imposing." She was so apologetic and I said, "No, no, not at all." She said, "I just wanted to give you this card." The card said that I had changed her life with my books. She's very apologetic and shy about it and I thought, I can't imagine anyone doing me a greater honor than what my readers do when they say my writing speaks to them or I changed their lives. They're not imposing but it's like, wow! It reached somebody.

I almost cried. I teared up. She walked away quickly so I was by myself by the time I was reading the card. It felt really, really good like, wow! It reaches somebody. It changed somebody's life in a good way. It just surprised me. I thought my crappy writing actually did something. I'm very hard on myself. I don't have a very high opinion of a lot of things I do. I think I'm lazy and I mess around and I don't do what I should do. I don't finish things when I should. Someone says something like that and it just gives you a little bit to keep you going.

Winning a Nebula, that was a high point. It was so funny. I was sure I wouldn't win. It was for *The Quantum Rose*, which is a very romantic book. I'm probably the only science fiction writer who's been nominated for the Hugo, the Nebula, and the RITA from the romance writers. It's a retelling of beauty and the beast. I thought there's no way this is going to win and it was going against Connie Willis and several brilliant hard science-fiction novels, one by Geoffrey Landis. I thought there's no way. I said Connie's going to win or Jeffrey's going to win so I didn't even write a speech or anything. I didn't bother. I did go to the ceremony because it's kind of fun to go and have people say, "Oh, you're a nominee." I'm sitting next to Nancy Kress and we're talking. She says, "Catherine, you ought to write something down." She said, "I didn't think I was going to win when I did, and I wrote something at the last minute because somebody told me to do it. So I'm going to tell you to write something." I said, "No, Nancy. Don't be silly. Nobody's going to vote for a romance for the Nebula." Nancy said, "Well you should do it anyway." I took my (name tag), turned it over and I scribbled some stuff on the back. They're doing the announcement. It's two people. They were kind of joking about the various nominees for novel and they said, "And there's Connie Willis and then there's these hard sci-fi writers." They didn't name me as one of the hard sci-fi writers. My agent was over there looking really mad because she knows how much criticism I got when I first started writing hard science fiction. It wasn't canonical, and because I'm a woman it got a lot of criticism. There are

romances in it or it wasn't so much that there was romance in it but there was a lot of touchy feely stuff about emotions that people didn't associate with hard science fiction. It was controversial when I first started. So when they didn't mention me she started looking kind of mad. I didn't care at that point. I was just waiting to hear who won. It had never occurred to me that they didn't mention me because I won.

Then they're going on and they say, "And the winner is Catherine Asaro for *The Quantum Rose*." I swear to god I just sat there with my mouth open. My agent was about to get up and come over and pull me out of my seat when finally Nancy kind of did this and I got up and I went up. Thank god she told me to write that because I was fumbling with my thing and I said, "Okay, Nancy Kress told me to write this." If it wasn't for her I would've just stood up there with my mouth open. I couldn't believe it. I mean I literally couldn't believe it.

It almost was like I couldn't process it. I just kind of, "What? Is this a mistake?" And you know—did you ever see that scene in the Olympics where all the runners run together? It's a really funny scene from the Olympics maybe ten, fifteen years ago. They all run together and they fall over. The guy who was behind them runs past them and wins the gold medal. That's what I felt like. They're all these really good people and they probably split the vote so I won. My agent was going, "No Catherine, it was a good book. Don't put yourself down." But that's what I felt like when I won.

It was an award given by my peers. It's the highest award science fiction has to give along with the Hugo Award, and it came from my peers. It was incredible. Maybe I wasn't as bad as I thought I was. I'm still not happy with the book but it is one of my better ones.

There's some sexual violence in my earlier stories that I just don't know if I'd put it in as explicitly now as I did then. I think I've changed and become more aware of the affect that such scenes can have. That they're more upsetting to some readers than I realized. They're triggers. I don't know if that's what I wanted to do, if my intent was to trigger certain reactions but it wasn't. I deal a lot with questions of role reversal, of violence, of gender issues. I'm not sure the methods I chose to deal with it were always the most successful to achieve what I wanted or—the comments that I wanted to make. I may not have made them so explicit. They are aspects of the stories. You can't deal with those kinds of issues without having them there to be dealt with. I think I would have made them less explicit. I think my writing now is a little bit less explicit than it used to be.

The writing is the most important. I do like running the Chesapeake Math Program. I like doing that but it does take time from the writing so it's a constant tension. My writing slowed down a lot since I started running this program. I want to write. That's really what I want to do but it's hard to walk away from something that you also very much like to do. I've made up stories since I was old enough to think. I started imagining alternate worlds when I was two or three years old. I've done it all my life. It's so much a part of what I am I don't know how I could do anything else.

JW: How do you want to be remembered?

CA: When I first started I didn't get a lot of acknowledgement for (hard science in my writing). I would get people saying, "Oh well, maybe she knows a little bit of physics." I have a doctorate from Harvard in this stuff.

Now, the world's changed. Even in the twenty, twenty-five years since I started, people are more willing to accept a woman in that role. I'd like to be remembered for that. I'd like to be remembered for starting a conversation on the representation of women and challenging literary gender roles. I think I was born a feminist and I grew up very aware of all these differences in how women and men were viewed. It was implicit in how I saw things and nobody else saw it. You know, I grew up in a world not long after the 1950s where father knows best and a strong female role model is Donna Reed. At the time, I respected her in the sense that she was the only woman who had a television story, she and Lucille Ball. They were not, in any way, role models that I wanted to emulate.

I wanted to go out in space and be the fighter pilot. I almost took that for granted, that that was a good thing to write about. I never had trouble writing about it, even though I grew up in a time when women did not do that. I mean period. There was no representation. I've seen the world change so much since then, it's become so much more accepted and I like to think that maybe I played a little bit of a role in making that happen. And I still enjoy writing those characters. I have more freedom now because there's less pressure not to do it. It's more accepted so I have more freedom in what people will publish. I think if I'm remembered for anything, I would be—I would be honored to be remembered for that. Maybe I made a little bit of a difference in the world.

Copyright © 2018 by Joy Ward

DAUGHTER OF ELYSIUM

SERIALIZATION
DAUGHTER OF ELYSIUM

CHAPTER 9

BY JOAN SLONCZEWSKI
Trade Paperback: 356 pages.
ISBN: 978-1-60450-444-6

While Raincloud handled simultaneously the Sharer negotiations and the latest Urulite crisis, Blackbear's work took a new direction. In the laboratory he had identified several novel mutants of his *Eyeless* gene. Two of them had control sequences that might prevent the early-onset heart disease in three-century-old Elysians. Pirin wanted to test them in simbrid embryos right away.

The call from his old clinic at Founders had renewed Blackbear's enthusiasm for his work. Let the Elysians shut down their fertility work—in the long run, it made little difference to him, because he would set up his own lab on Bronze Sky. The main thing was to learn as many techniques as he could while he was here with the experts.

The simbrid embryo testing would be crucial, whatever problem he chose to work on. So he might as well work with Pirin on the *Eyeless* mutants. Their goal was to replace the *Eyeless* sequence on simbrid chromosome seven with one of Blackbear's mutant sequences, then watch the embryo develop—normally, they hoped.

"How much DNA will you need?" Blackbear asked. He could program the synthesizer to build any mutant gene, a few thousand copies at a time.

Pirin considered this. "How many base pairs of your mutant differ from the parental sequence?"

"Twenty-three positions differ, over a region of three hundred bases."

"That's not too bad," said Pirin. "Instead of cutting out and splicing the whole region, we'll send in a molecular servo to modify each base chemically."

That made sense. The four different nucleotide bases, or "letters" of the DNA alphabet, were chemically interchangeable except for the inward-pointing tab of each structure. The inward-pointing portions, which determined the DNA sequence, could be converted by adding or removing methyl and amino groups; rather like changing a c to an e by adding a stroke.

So the two of them spent the next half hour programming the molecular servos to perform the correct series of reactions, at the correct base positions. Since each servo could store only eight operations (there were atomic limits, after all) three servos had to be programmed, which took longer than Pirin had thought. But by the afternoon they were ready to put the servos into the fertilized egg cell to modify the chromosomal DNA.

They watched the tabletop holostage as it formed the image of the transparent egg. Within the sphere of granular cytoplasm, the two pronuclei were suspended, one each from the egg and from the disintegrated sperm which had fertilized it. Each pronucleus contained the parental chromosomes entwined inside, decondensed and invisible at this magnification.

From across the table Hawktalon leaned over to get a better look, her braids sparkling as they caught some of the light. "Daddy, did I really look like that once?"

He blinked, taken aback. "You certainly did." Seven standard years ago that was, eight counting gestation. I'm getting old, Blackbear thought.

"Fertilization is not yet complete," Pirin pointed out. "It will take several hours before the pronuclear membranes dissolve and the chromosomes migrate together. At that point, the chromosomes will condense for the first cell division. Once condensed, the chromosomes will be impenetrable. So we need to get the servos inside now."

At Pirin's spoken command, two microscopic needles pierced the cell, one for each pronucleus. Each needle pulled three molecular servos into the pronucleus. Of course, the servos could not be "seen" at this resolution, but the holostage gradually focused in. First the cytoplasm, with its reticulum of molecular transport enlarged, then fell away as the bubble of the nucleus expanded to fill the stage. Then the nuclear membranes and most of the chromosomes expanded out of range. "We need more contrast," Pirin said. Another command, and the elegant curves of a DNA helix snaked across a foglike background. Blackbear made a mental note of this command.

"Do the servos find their own way to the proper gene sequence on the chromosome?" Blackbear wondered.

"That's what we'll find out," said Pirin. "They should; they're all programmed for that. Here we've focused on the *Eyeless* sequence. It shouldn't take long for the servos to show up."

Hawktalon asked, "Is that really a DNA gene?" She sounded disappointed. "Where are all the oxygens and nitrogens?"

"Atoms aren't really colored balls on a stick," Blackbear reminded her. "They're just fuzzy clouds of electrons."

Pirin looked up. "They can be colored balls, if you'd like." At a command, the DNA turned into a winding collage of blue oxygens, red nitrogens, and tiny black hydrogens dotting the zigzag skeleton of carbon atoms.

"What's that crawling alongside?" Hawktalon put her hand into the image. A chain of atoms shaped like a leech with a sucker on each end was creeping end-over-end along the major groove of the double helix. At one point it slowed to a halt, tapped several times about the groove, then settled and rearranged itself.

Pirin said, "That's the nanoservo. It's sitting at a cytosine base, the first one you wanted to mutate. The servo will replace the cytosine's amino group with a hydroxyl, which immediately isomerizes to the ketone of thymine, the transformed base."

Before Blackbear could speak, Hawktalon added, "You need an extra methyl group, too, to make thymine."

"That's right." Pirin looked at her, rather surprised.

"She does her homework," Blackbear said proudly. Then he frowned, puzzled. "Something doesn't make sense about this. How can we 'see' all these molecules, as if they just sit there? Don't they vibrate constantly, in Brownian motion?"

"Of course, molecules are never stationary, just as their atoms are not red and blue balls. What you 'see' here is a time-averaged representation of their electron density."

Everything was a "representation," at this level; nothing was what it seemed. Blackbear stretched himself, feeling vaguely disoriented to be immersed so deep in the realm of the unseen and untouchable. He remembered the surgical ward of the clinic, where reality was as concrete as a swollen worm of an appendix for his fingers to find and remove.

Then he had an idea. "You know, now that I'm getting into this project, I'd like to research the heart syndromes some more."

"I'll give you some papers to read," said Pirin.

"I'd like to interview patients, too."

"We have every patient on file, from holo recording to molecular composition of all their bodily fluids."

"Great; that will help when I interview them."

Pirin looked at him oddly. "Excuse me?"

Blackbear hesitated. His command of Elysian was fairly good by now. "I mean, visit the patients—talk with them, examine them. That way I'll get a real feel for the disease; I might find some lost connections."

"Oh, I see." Pirin shuddered. "I suppose you could. Perhaps the … Perhaps Tulle might arrange it. I'm not sure what good it would do. We're working at the molecular level, after all. Excuse me, I have another experiment to attend to."

Astonished, Blackbear watched the Elysian student depart, his talar hung precisely across his smooth unblemished back. At the Founders clinic, even the research specialists regularly toured their wards. But here, he had not seen a patient in months. For that matter, he had never seen a sick Elysian.

By the next morning, each mutant egg cell had cleaved successfully into two identical cells. The twin speckled ovals hugged together, each with its nucleus like a crystalline marble floating inside. Blackbear watched, feeling a peculiar sense of beauty and shame, as if it might be a sacrilege to watch the work of the Goddess unfold under such a battery of instruments.

The next few cell divisions would each require most of a day to complete. They could not be "sped up," as in the simulator, so there was nothing to do but wait for development to proceed over the next several months. By the third month, most serious defects would likely have appeared.

In three months Raincloud would be on Urulan—unless they called it off after this latest freighter attack. Blackbear shuddered. It did him no good to have so much time on his hands to think about things.

He needed to see patients. It had been such a relief to see the last of them, yet now he longed for someone to reassure with a kind word, or bring comfort with the right dosage. He needed to feel like a doctor again. He might not yet know enough to convince Pirin, but he could not escape the conviction that any approach from his lab had to connect somehow with actual patients.

From outside came Sunflower's delighted peals of laughter. The toybox must have come up with something new to entertain him.

Something tugged at Blackbear's trouser leg. Startled, he drew back from the egg in its nanoplastic womb and looked quickly down. He half expected Blueskywind, who loved to lie on her tummy and tug at anyone within reach. But of course the baby was off with Raincloud, helping negotiate with the Sharers.

It was Tulle's capuchin trying to stick her nose beneath the hem of his trouser leg. The capuchin found his trousers a source of amusement; somehow she always seemed to think they must hide a treat somewhere, like one of Tulle's pockets. Blackbear scooped the animal up and sat her on his hand, showing her the newly divided egg. "See there, little devil," he told her. "What do you think? You once looked like that, too."

The capuchin scampered down as Tulle entered the lab. "I hear all your eggs took," said Tulle.

"So far," Blackbear agreed. "We had to reinject the servos on one of them, but now they've all reached the two-cell stage."

"Great start," said Tulle. "If I were you, though, I'd try a couple of gene replacements, too. I know Pirin likes point mutations, but if the servos make one mistake, you waste months of development."

"I see. Well, I'll set one up then; I certainly need to learn that technique, too."

"Pirin tells me you'd like to look at the disease in human patients."

"Well," he said guardedly, "I thought it might be useful."

"It's a very good idea," she said. "We need to broaden our approach. The machines don't know everything. I'll make us an appointment at the Palace of Health."

The Palace of Health was not in Helicon. It was located inside a large disk-shaped satellite that orbited the planet. The satellite's rotation generated near-normal g-force at its outer rim. As Blackbear entered from the shuttlecraft, with Tulle and Pirin and the children, the first thing they did, of course, was to meditate at the butterfly garden. Blackbear left the children off at the garden with Doggie, with a holocube in Hawktalon's hand and strict instructions to keep in contact with Dad.

Finding the entrance within the upcurving tunnel of the ring's outer rim was a bit of a puzzle. Even Tulle seemed to have trouble locating a door with her groping hand. Pirin, who took his role as senior student very seriously, had dutifully come along but he hung back now, as if hoping Tulle might not find the door.

"May we enter please?" Tulle spoke at last, giving up.

The palest outline of a doorway appeared, just a glimmer of light tracing its arch. Above the portal a faint inscription appeared, in fancy Elysian letters similar to the inscription above Science Park. With some difficulty Blackbear made it out; not "Hope Abandons," as he first thought, but "Hope Follows All Who Enter Here."

From the top of the arch a furrow deepened and extended down to the threshold, as if the double doors were about to open. Then a servo voice spoke. "You are expected, Citizens, but one of you has no psychiatric exam on file."

"He's a foreigner," explained Tulle. "Foreigners don't require the exam. They're used to morbidity."

A moment passed. "You are correct. Please report my defect to …"

The doors parted, folds of nanoplast wrinkling along their inner edge. An attendant came to meet them, a blank-faced servo built somewhat like a waiter, wearing white instead of black. "This way, please," the attendant spoke in the soothing tones of a shuttlecraft. "The first patient on your list inhabits a chamber with oxygen-enriched atmosphere. You will remain outside; however, if physical examination is required, I can assist."

The patient's chamber was located at an "upper" level, an inner ring of the satellite where the artificial g-force was so low that the visitors had to use handholds to steady themselves. They found themselves looking down at a sizable chamber of glass, within which a woman sat upon a floating cushion. From her shoulders a train of swallowtails drifted around her in a haphazard spiral. Arlen Papili*shon* was the name Blackbear had memorized from her file. The lowered g-force in her chamber was intended to reduce the strain on her heart, which had atrophied despite repeated transplants.

"Good morning, doctors." From a speaker somewhere, Arlen's firm voice replaced that of the hospital. "I hear the highest reports of you," she added, for Pirin had dutifully called up the *generen* of each patient; few of them seemed to have mates. She rose from her seat and floated slowly upward toward them. Her eyes blinked rapidly, as if a sudden light irritated them. She was very thin, but appeared otherwise healthy and alert, her skin as smooth as Blueskywind's.

The hospital told her, "You will be asked to undress for examination."

"Undress? Now there's something I haven't been asked in a long time," said Arlen ironically, "not by a human, at any rate."

"I'd like to ask a few questions first," said Blackbear. He could already see the obvious: the distended neck veins, the shortness of breath, and other symptoms typical of cardiomyopathy. "I'm Doctor Windclan; my mate will hear the highest reports. We're researchers, you know, trying to cure and prevent your type of heart disorder."

"Oh, you're Doctor Windclan. I've already heard all about you, from Kal Anaea*shon*. He visits me every week."

At that, all his questions flew out of his head. Flustered, he turned over a page in his notes, trying to avoid the eyes of his colleagues. "Uh, could you tell me, first off, how's your digestion?" He asked what she thought of her diet, whether she slept well, whether she had chest pains. Beside her a beverage cup and a holocube gradually descended. As the patient answered his questions, a jumble of figures from her file passed through his head: her pulse rate was high, her heart chambers were atrophied and misshapen, her blood contained abnormal cardiac enzymes, and several of the thirty-six different classes of white cells were low. Blackbear relaxed and felt quite the physician again, while Tulle and Pirin stood by listening.

"Is there anything at all that bothers you," Blackbear asked the woman, "aside from your heart? Any aches, joint stiffness, anything?"

"I ache to get out of here." Her eyes blinked rapidly again.

A rush of recollection came over him, for how many patients on the chronic ward at Founders would have said the same. He regarded her with warm sympathy. "What about your eyes?" he asked. "Any vision problems?"

"No, but I will have if they keep the light this bright forever. I don't know why the light's so bright in here."

The hospital told Blackbear, "The patient exhibits certain delusions; see her file."

"Well you could still check her eyes out," Blackbear replied.

"It will be done, Doctor."

"A pleasure meeting you, Doctor Windclan," Arlen called out to him. "Do stop by again, one of these decades. Or send your great-grandson, someday." For generations she could float there in that near-weightless balloon.

When the exam was completed, the attendant led them away toward the next patient, catching the handholds one by one. For a minute or so, the three researchers were silent. Blackbear recalled Kal's offer, to take him to visit the "defective" Elysians.

"That Kal," said Pirin scornfully. "How like him, to prefer the dead to the living."

"But that patient's *not* dead," Blackbear exclaimed. "With all your transplantation technology, why can't she be cured?"

Pirin looked offended. "Nothing's perfect."

"You saw her file," Tulle reminded him. "She's had half a dozen transplants. They all go bad. Some regulator response is messed up, something outside the heart that acts upon it. That's just what you're trying to work put."

"Where do all these transplanted organs come from?" he wondered. "You don't seem to have all the transit crashes that we do back home."

At that, Pirin gave him a very odd look indeed. "The organs come from simbrid embryos, of course."

He froze in his tracks. So Elysians grew up those near-human fetuses for more than medical research. Human enough to transplant, but not enough to be born as infants.

Tulle paused, looking back to him.

"I was just wondering," Blackbear said, as he walked on more slowly, "whatever would happen if one of those simbrids happened to be 'born.'"

"That couldn't happen," said Pirin. "Anyway, it would only produce an indecent sort of animal."

"It might be intelligent."

Pirin laughed. "Intelligence isn't everything. Servos are intelligent."

Tulle considered this. Beyond her, the blank-faced attendant was about to introduce the next patient. "Society needs limits," she said quietly. "We make sure the simbrids aren't born, for the same reason we cleanse our servos."

CHAPTER 10

The loss of the second Valan ship filled the news for over a week. Since no actual footage was available from this latest event, the news replayed old recordings of Imperial nuclear attacks on their provinces, in case anyone needed a reminder of Urulite savagery.

In a surprise appearance, Lord Zheron broadcast a speech across the Fold. Now elevated to the post of Imperial Grand Vizier, Zheron gave a remarkably frank account of the incident. "The Imperator had not the slightest intent to harm a single Valan barbarian on their stinking spy ship. Our regional commander of the Imperial Fleet was under orders only to follow the ship until it passed well beyond Imperial space territory. Unfortunately, a rogue ship of an enemy of the Imperium destroyed the Valan spy ship, intending to discredit His August Majesty the Imperator. The inhuman perpetrators of this treasonous deed will be eliminated! That is, brought to trial."

Inside Verid's office, the statement with its translation floated in bright letters above the table. Raincloud was pointing out the nuances. "An 'enemy of the Imperium' generally means a personal enemy of the Imperator," she noted.

Lem nodded. "Not surprising, given all the claimants Rhaghlan had to eliminate. They must have hundreds of supporters still at large."

The three of them reflected silently on the implications for stability of the new regime.

"Was it really a spy ship?" Lem asked.

Verid shrugged. "Any Valan ship passing so close to Urulite space probably carries a spy or two."

"So what are the Valans going to do about it?"

"They've already demanded a session of the Fold Council to authorize a space blockade. This can be done by generating white holes at those jump stations essential for Urulite vessels to cross the Fold."

Raincloud blinked. "But if Urulan is closed off, how will we be able to—"

Both Verid and Lem stared at her, hands raised. No one was to mention the Urulan trip, even in the security of Verid's office.

"Of course it would make no practical difference," Verid said loudly, "since no one in the Fold visits Urulan. Nonetheless, given our Elysian emphasis on the long-term view, we would prefer a more judicious response." She waved a hand above the table, and the floating letters disappeared. "I think I'll handle the Valan demands. A few minor Valan indiscretions might come to light; we save them for just such occasions. Now, about our friends at Kshiri-el. Any progress?"

With difficulty Raincloud shifted gears in her head. She had spent her last couple of days at Kshiri-el "negotiating" with Yshri, while studying Urulite documents all night; it was enough to make her head spin. "Mostly all Yshri wants to talk about is how people could lifeshape themselves for a new planet," she summarized. "Then Ooruwen comes in and tells us it's hopeless, and nothing but total abandonment of the project will do." Ooruwen was just as capable of colorful language as Zheron. "I get the feeling there are as many opinions on this as there are Sharers."

Verid grinned, and her shoulders shook as she chuckled. "I think you know our good sisters well. Still, it's a shame that Leresha won't come back to talk. She would have woven something together."

Considering Leresha's views, Raincloud thought that whatever she wove together would be unlikely to please the Elysians.

The Fold Council declined to block Urulan's jump stations, but they called for monetary compensation. The figure demanded was high, and the vote passed by a large margin; only Elysium abstained, to the withering scorn of Valedon and other Fold members.

From Urulan, the demand met silence. Well deserved though it was, Raincloud suspected even a tenth that amount might be hard for the impoverished Imperium to come up with.

Over the next two months, Raincloud spent more and more of her Visiting Days inside the high-force satellite, training with Lem and Iras. With regular medical treatment, her muscles swelled to an alarming extent; her sleeves no longer fit, and she felt afraid to hug the children, lest she squeeze too hard.

"Enough of this," she told Iras one day as they swung their arms before practice. "I know those Urulites grow biceps to rival Black Elbow, but any more will just block my movements."

"I've noticed that." Iras had grown her flesh a bit, too, although not so much as Lem, who had allowed his thighs and upper arms to expand until he looked almost gross.

"Let's work on multiple attacks today," said Raincloud. Even with her added muscle mass, an Urulite fighter could well outweigh her twice over, so the best she could do to simulate was to take on two at once. "We'll start with an easy one. You both grab my arms from the front, aiming to pin me. I'll respond with a hip pull, and you'll both end up on your backs on the floor."

Iras thought it over. "I see, a double 'Falling Leaves.'"

Lem still looked skeptical, but the two of them stepped into position. Raincloud bent at the knees to lower her center of gravity and let her shoulders relax. This would take concentration; thank Goddess the two of them were good enough by now so that she no longer had to worry how they fell.

They sprang at her at once, each catching one of her forearms, which she had carefully turned down. She bent low, her hips moving back, while her arms swung theirs into alignment together. Then her torso thrust swiftly forward beneath the four arms; a pivot to the right propelled the arms back, still along their original path of momentum. The attackers' bodies naturally followed their arms, rotating to fall on their backs on the mat. A resounding thud echoed through the practice room. Raincloud finished the move by twisting both their arms to the mat, taking care to keep them intertwined. The "leaves" had "fallen," all right. For a moment there was silence, filled only by her heart pounding heavily inside.

"Great job," said Raincloud enthusiastically. "You both fell just right. You really know what you're doing now."

"Do you think so?" Iras asked, as she got herself up and clapped the dust off her hands. "Will we put on a good show for our … friends?"

Raincloud considered this. The Elysians had trained at an astonishing rate, to within two levels of the top form reached by a Clicker goddess, perhaps within one level in the case of Iras. Raincloud took care to avoid teaching Lem certain moves which only a goddess was supposed to know; it might make no difference here, but she was still traditional about some things. At any rate, she had little doubt that they could show their Urulite hosts a thing or two. "I think that … Hyen's friends will be impressed."

To explain their activities to the public, Hyen had scheduled the three of them for a private exhibition at the *Houris* the week after their secret trip. The sleazier news networks were already speculating.

The next month passed with little movement in Sharer negotiations, but in Helicon there were disquieting signs. The streets were not quite so clean as usual; in fact, they were marred by little tumbleweeds that seemed to have come from nowhere. The tumbleweeds rarely grew larger than one's fist, but their tough interlocked branches caught in trains and in hair, and they clogged even the streetcleaners.

"They multiply faster than the cleaners can be unclogged," Iras told Raincloud. "At this rate, they'll smother the butterfly gardens. Let's hope Verid does something."

Raincloud was surprised. "What's Verid got to do with it?"

"Why, it's a 'gift' from the Sharers, of course. Just like the fruit flies—their classic tactic."

"Yshri wouldn't do such a thing." But even as she spoke, Raincloud knew that Iras was right. Enough Sharers on other rafts were still mad at Helicon. The "negotiations" were useless without their support.

At home, Blueskywind could creep across the floor with surprising speed, especially when she caught sight of her favorite rubber squid. The squid was a gift from Draeg, a typical tourist toy from Shora. It was just the right size for her to stuff it between her gums, mouthing it all over, limbs and all.

Awake now most of the day, the baby babbled incessantly, long "Ah-ahs" and trills. Once she caught on to the "click" sound of the Clicker language, it caught her fancy for some reason, more than it had for her siblings. She practiced the click and exaggerated it, with Hawktalon's encouragement, until it became a loud "Pop!" as she pulled her tongue out from the palate under pressure. When put down to nap, she would "pop" noisily to amuse herself until at last she fell asleep—much to her parents' relief.

From Bronze Sky Nightstorm wrote that Falcon Soaring had her baby; that is, Raincloud's sister Lynxtail had given birth two months before, and by ritual of the Goddess had transferred the child to her cousin. The news reopened a wound, leaving Raincloud depressed. Blackbear worried more about the fire season. The fires were lasting longer than usual, in an exceptionally dry year, and had already claimed half of Tumbling Rock. His own brothers' village kept a nightly watch, just in case the fire burned their way and they would have to flee to Crater Lake.

Snake Day came again, just one Bronze Skyan year since they arrived in Helicon. Hawktalon dressed up the Goddess figure in paper snakes, and, much to her delight, Raincloud had actually borrowed a real live blacksnake from Tulle's preserve. It must have fed not long before; it hung itself torpidly along the black glazed arms, flicking its tongue now and then.

The trip to Urulan, disguised as a staff retreat, was less than a week off now, unnervingly near. Blackbear gave her one of his dark looks. "You're still going?"

Raincloud clenched her hands. "I can hardly dishonor the Snake." Since the latest freighter "accident," Blackbear was dead set against her going; the fact that they could not discuss Urulan directly only made things worse.

Verid called her in for one last review of their protocols and their negotiating plan. The two conferred on a ship in the outskirts of the solar system, where security could be maximized.

"The opening script is clear," Verid reminded her. "Zheron expects you to fight the Imperial Champion 'to the death.' I tried to get this part waived, but he insisted on it."

"I understand." The Elysians would not have to risk their millennial bodies. "At least it's not the Imperator himself; since he's a 'god,' I would have to lose."

"The ship will have full medical facilities. But don't push it, by Helix; I'll need you afterward in one piece!"

She smiled ruefully. "I'll do my best."

"Keep in mind," Verid said, "our main aim is to find out what they want, what they think they need, to make peace with the Fold."

"And commit them to disarmament."

"If possible; we'll see how much we can do in one visit. Remember, this encounter will be a big shock to the common Urulites. To face something as big as the Fold—bigger than their gods."

Raincloud had some idea what that meant. She recalled Nightstorm's remarks about "chromosomes."

"The young Imperator is the key to everything," Verid added. "He has to want to work with us."

She nodded. "Rhaghlan wants peace and trade, and even democracy someday. He will liberate women and slaves."

"He opposes abortion, though," Verid added. "He gave a whole speech about that. Are you sure he meant 'abortion'? Our previous translators would have rendered that 'baby-killing.'"

"Urulites do not distinguish between the two," Raincloud explained. "If a man's wife conceives a child whom he can't support, or if he doubts its paternity, he may order it terminated before birth, or after birth he may hold it under water, to preserve his honor. Since females have no honor, they are not permitted to do this."

Verid thought a moment. "So for Rhaghlan to oppose 'baby-killing' is rather enlightened."

"I wish all his views were so enlightened. He remains rather obsessed with 'pure blood,'" Raincloud pointed out. "There are reports that he has imprisoned and possibly executed people for questioning his own godly descent."

"That's unfortunate, but not surprising," Verid said. "His mother, though a lady of high rank, was not a queen; his enemies are bound to exploit it."

For some minutes the two fell silent. They had gone over everything so many times.

"Raincloud, I want you to leave the baby home."

She stared, for a moment breathless at this sudden turn. "We had that settled," she exclaimed. "I told you, I can't let her go without nursing. You said she could come, so long as she stays with Iras while I'm on duty." Iras's nominal role on the trip was to "introduce" Verid, as her mate; on the side, Raincloud figured, she would scout out business prospects.

"I know," Verid said, "but I've had second thoughts about nonprofessional participants. This Imperator may mean well, but he can't guarantee our safety."

"Only Elysians would expect that," said Raincloud with frank disgust. "The baby goes where I go."

"Your mate feels differently."

At that Raincloud was too enraged for words. How dared Verid spy on her at home with Blackbear. She took a deep breath. "Your own mate disagrees with you," she said coldly. "Yet *she's* coming."

Verid looked away. "Iras will stay home, if your baby does."

Now Raincloud understood. Verid feared for Iras, too. "Let Iras stay home, and live a thousand years. My daughter has her honor to think of."

CHAPTER 11

The spaceship had the same close-fit quarters as the ship that had carried the Windclans out from Bronze Sky. Raincloud could scarcely escape the sense that she was heading home, instead of toward the dreaded Urulan. "Little Lushaywen," she whispered in Sharer to her wide-eyed child. "How could I ever have imagined then what sort of journey we'd share now?"

The baby felt heavy in her arms, for the ship had already set its gravity to Urulite standard. The extra acceleration would speed their journey, too, though it made little difference nowadays. From the travelers' perspective, their trip would take barely a day, mostly at near-lightspeed, with a jump station every hour or so. Back at Shora, over a week would elapse; then another week, after their three-day stay. Of course she could not have left the baby so long.

Still, better a week than twenty years. The Heliconians long ago had discovered that this lobe of the galaxy, called the Fold, was multiply folded on top of itself in one of its twenty-three dimensions, rather like a scarf folded up in a pocket. A jump station was a place where sufficient energy was concentrated to poke a hole across the fold, like a needle poking through a fold of the scarf. Today modern ships could thread in and out of the jump stations, taking shortcuts all the way to Solaria, a world on the farthest edge of the Fold.

"Last chance for second thoughts, Citizens," Verid announced as they reached their final jump station.

Lem laughed. "Wasn't this the one the Valans tried to shut down?"

Raincloud frowned at the heavy-handed jest. Then she turned her baby over to the nana for a diaper change.

The jump station appeared as an elliptical shape, absolutely black against the stars. Once the ship entered, it would start to spin at an exceptional rate, and the interior would experience high g-forces. So, as usual, all passengers reported to the central axis of the ship where they would strap down in order to pass through safely. Raincloud strapped her baby down, too; a bit of a trick in the near-weightless condition, but after all her travels she had grown accustomed to the straps and buckles floating off unpredictably, and the sense of confusion in her inner ears. She settled back calmly and stretched. A holostage was situated conveniently to provide what passed for Elysian entertainment.

The transition began smoothly enough. As the pressure increased, like a hand pushing her back, she took deep, regular breaths. The pressure gradually reached its maximum, about three or four g's she guessed.

But instead of declining, the pressure rose again. The hand on her chest was now a lead blanket grinding her cruelly into the cushions that were supposed to protect her. She strained for air and tried to cry out for her child, but no sound escaped. An oxygen mask came over her face; that was the last she remembered.

When she revived, she ached in every muscle. Servo medics hovered over her and the other passengers, whisking tubes and sniffers here and there. Blueskywind was screaming at the top of her lungs, probably because she felt as sore as her mother did. Raincloud tried to calm her down enough to nurse. That jump was a bad one.

"Emergency alert, Citizens." The ship itself was one great servo, which piloted itself without human assistance. "This jump station has not been well maintained; a gravitational anomaly stressed our equipment on passing through. The craft has sustained significant damage."

The passengers exchanged looks. Iras caught Raincloud's sleeve to reassure her.

Verid asked, "Will we be able to get back out again after our mission?"

"I can't say for sure," the ship told her. "I will run all necessary checks."

"Good," Verid snapped. "Inform me as soon as possible, please."

Lem was no longer laughing. "Those primitive bastards," he muttered. "They can't even keep up their jump stations."

"Well what do you expect, with the Fold boycott against them?" asked Raincloud.

"Exactly," Verid agreed. "It's a wonder they keep up anything at all."

Iras was watching the viewscreen. Her lips parted, and she pointed at a small yellow disk that stood out against the field of stars. "Is that … ?"

"That is Urulan's sun," the ship confirmed. "One point two standard mass, spectral range—"

"Very well," Verid interrupted. "Any contact from our host yet?"

"Not yet."

"Satellites out?"

"The satellites have been launched, Citizen." The spy satellites were to be released immediately to count Urulan's missiles—before Zheron or anyone else might change his mind. "Warning," the ship added, "my sensors already detect traces of radionuclear debris. If these emanate from the planet Urulan, my calculations suggest you will all require cancer prophylaxis."

"Great Helix," muttered Lem. "We're visiting a graveyard."

"Contact!" called the ship. "An approaching vessel requests immediate contact—'

"Granted," Verid quickly replied.

Before the viewscreen, the holostage filled with light. An image wove in and out, then settled at last.

It was Lord Zheron, as big as life. The burly oversized dwarf of a man had changed little; his blue tunic was layered over with chain mail, and weapons of every description bristled from his belt. He slapped his leg emphatically. "Lord Raincloud! You owe me one," he reminded her. "I'm onto your tricks; you won't get me outside the ring again."

Verid cleared her throat. "Grand Vizier," she greeted him carefully. "It is an honor to meet you once more."

"His Majesty the Imperator awaits you. Prepare ships for docking."

A phalanx of octopods emerged from the back of the Elysian ship, mainly to impress the natives, Raincloud thought. Zheron could easily obliterate their ship if he chose. As the two ships locked on, the nana came back with Blueskywind.

Raincloud turned to Iras.

"I'll take good care of her." Iras had some knack with babies, after her years with Verid at the *shon*. Meanwhile, Raincloud figured that since she herself was the designated "male" for this trip, she had best leave the little one to others at least until after their royal introductions. What a sight one of those Urulites would make if he suddenly found himself in Tumbling Rock—childless, and bristling with silly pointed things. How the goddesses would laugh and speculate as to why he needed more than one.

Zheron's soldiers soon boarded, all of them about Elysian height yet twice as wide, their eyes bright blue, their hair straight and sand-colored. Zheron himself and his weapons master, Lord Dhesra, now the Imperial Master Armorer, both clapped her on the shoulder and exclaimed at how long ago they had last seen her. Raincloud recalled Dhesra's frank remarks on what ought to become of certain Imperial retainers.

The soldiers' search of the vessel took longer than expected, in part because they seemed intensely curious about even the most mundane details of the Elysian ship, down to the little cleaner servos that scurried out to wipe the dust from their shoes. The men smelled as if they could use a cleaning, too. At any rate, Raincloud took the chance to sneak in one more nursing of the baby before she fell asleep. Caressing Blueskywind's forehead one last time, she handed her over to Iras. The three of them rejoined Verid and Lem as they transferred to Zheron's ship, leaving their own ship to park above Urulan's equator.

The Urulite interior reeked of must and machine oil, and other smells best left unidentified. The floor hummed unnervingly underfoot. The bridge was full of manual switches and packed with men slamming controls and shouting back at the instruments when they disliked the response. Nonetheless, Zheron was immensely proud of his vessel, and he insisted on giving the Elysians a full tour, thumping the back of each crew member as he announced his job. Raincloud caught a glimpse of Lem's face, rather pale; she suspected he felt sick.

By the time they reached the viewscreen, Urulan itself was in view: a lovely orb with patches of continent and ocean free of cloud, like Valedon, only greener. The Elysians transferred to a shuttle and descended through the atmosphere, a greenish sky gathering above them.

Below rose the famous "needle rocks" of Urulan. The dark brown mountains jutted spectacularly out of a dense green ground cover, casting shadows for several kilometers. Even though she had known intellectually what to expect, Raincloud's heart pounded harder the nearer they came.

All the while they descended, she translated for Zheron as he held forth on the past two millennia of Imperial history, starting with the birth of the first Imperator to the gods Azhragh and Mirhiah. Most of the history was familiar to Raincloud from her studies with Rhun; the few unfamiliar details she suspected were made up for the occasion. The shuttle was even more cramped than the spaceship had been, and as Zheron gesticulated, his arm occasionally brushed the chain mail of the pilot, who was doing his best to bring them in for a safe landing.

Suddenly Zheron flung out his arm toward the window. "Look there, below—a 'caterpillar.' You've heard, yes? One of our native fauna welcomes you to Urulan!"

Raincloud looked. A dense canopy of foliage could be seen, and she could just make out something moving.

Zheron pounded the pilot on the back. "Give them a closer look, will you?"

The shuttle dipped and swayed. Raincloud felt her stomach float up toward her lungs; she swallowed hard and gripped her armrests. The ground expanded and loomed upward toward them, until individual trees could be made out.

There it was, a "caterpillar," a monster like two elephants back-to-back with seven pairs of limbs in all. As if on purpose, its front two limbs happened to lift up just then, giving a full view of the caterpillar's mandibles; for a moment the shuttle seemed about to fall into them. Then the craft zoomed upward, tugging at her seat until it leveled off once more in the relative safety of the sky.

Raincloud took a deep breath. Reaching over, she gently caressed a black curl on the forehead of her daughter, sound asleep on Iras's shoulder. Behind her Lem's pale face had turned green.

The Imperial City of Azure arose upon a cluster of the needle rocks, linked together by delicate arched bridges that traced pale blue against the clear sky. The palace buildings consisted of round turrets with ledges that wound upward around them, like spiral ramps. Gold leaf lined the edges which caught the sunlight, winking in and out.

Below the city, farmlands descended in terraces, ending abruptly at a stone wall that traversed the girth of each needle rock. Only the surface of each needle rock had been treated for human agriculture. Eyeing those few precious bits of soil on slopes so steep even Clickers would hesitate to till, Raincloud guessed that Urulites might well wonder where their next meal would come from, for all the gold on their palaces.

The shuttle landed with surprising grace; that pilot must have known his business after all. An icy wind whipped across the grass, enough to make her welcome her goatskin jacket. Two columns of guards saluted them with horns. The guards rode Urulite llamas, sleepy-eyed beasts with long necks and elephantine legs, specially bred to withstand high gravity. A cart drawn by llamas drove up to bear the visitors to the Central Palace. The road was steep and full of cracked flagstones. The beasts' performance impressed Raincloud. She could use some of that stock in her fields back in Tumbling Rock.

When they reached the Central Palace, no one needed to be told. The structure was hard to believe, despite all the images Raincloud had seen. Gold covered all the outer wall and spiral ledge, with countless figures of the gods worked in bas-relief, inlaid with turquoise. Raincloud blinked and had to look away as the reflected sunlight hit her eyes. Only as the visitors approached closer could she see that some of the gold leaf was flaking off without replacement, and that ominous pockmarks marred the wall.

The carts stopped. Dhesra muttered, "This guard will show you to the ladies' quarter."

Taking her cue, Iras stepped out with the baby, an octopod behind her. Raincloud anxiously watched them disappear behind the Palace.

An enormous pair of double doors swung back, on hinges thicker than Raincloud's arm. As they dismounted from their cart with their octopods, Verid and Lem unfolded their trains, shortened to avoid need of trainsweeps. Zheron and Dhesra led them all into the Hall of the Azure Throne.

Zheron's demeanor underwent a marked change, Raincloud noticed. He seemed tense as a drawn bow, his eyes turning back and forth as if alert to the slightest deviation from protocol. Footsteps echoed on the marble floor as they strode forward between the lines of warriors. At either side of the hall rose columns covered with ornate decoration. She noticed, though, that some of the corners could have used a good cleaning, and that fissures and discolorations marked the floor.

They crossed the hall, nearing the black edge of the traditional Ring of Death. Behind the ring stood the Azure Throne, pale blue stone with golden symbols full of countless ancient meanings. Vessels of incense at either side released exotic odors. Beyond the throne rose richly patterned curtains; Raincloud guessed that the higher ranked ladies of the court waited behind.

A salute of drums and horns announced the pending entrance of the Imperator. At this point, visitors normally were supposed to bow low to the ground until the royal personage took his seat. The Elysians had debated for hours whether or not to do so, given the democratic principles of the Fold in general and Elysium in particular. At last they had settled on a limited bow from the waist, approximating the Elysian gesture of respect; Zheron had assented, observing with irritation that if Elysians all had bad backs, he would have to make allowances.

So Raincloud bowed, while Verid and Lem beside her did the same. Then she looked up.

In the throne sat a man who looked just like her old teacher Rhun. There was no mistaking the thin lips, the huge dark brow, the forehead sloping up into coarse black hair. Imperator Rhaghlan was a sim.

Raincloud froze as she stared. For a moment time seemed to stand still. Rhun—and yet not Rhun, of course, not the ghost from her past. A sim nonetheless; by the Goddess, how did he manage to keep the throne? No wonder that devil Zheron had blustered about blood.

She caught herself, hoping her shock had not registered. Of course, she was an idiot, for Zheron had warned them in his own inimitable way.

Beside her Verid and Lem kept admirable composure. Some sort of announcement was being made, which she hurried to interpret for them. Just how many Urulites had simian blood in their veins …

"In the name of the Urulite Imperium," Lord Dhesra was saying, "the Imperial Champion challenges the barbarian Lord Raincloud to fight to the death!"

A giant of a man entered the marble Ring of Death. Tall even by Bronze Skyan standards, his girth was like that of a tree trunk. There was no trace of sim in him. His back was erect, his face round, and his eyes blue as twin moons.

"Choose your weapons, Barbarian Lord," added Dhesra.

Raincloud exchanged a quick look with Verid. Verid's eyes were impassive. She replied, her voice reverberating strangely in the vast hall. "In the name of the *peaceful* people of Elysium, I ask for spirit only."

Soldiers muttered at this, and one of them banged his spear on the floor as if to object. It occurred to her, these men might never before have heard the name Elysium in the context of peace. Still, their leaders ought to have prepared them better. It was hardly a good sign.

The Champion merely nodded and handed his own sword and particle blaster to an attendant. Raincloud swiftly sized him up. Perhaps three times her weight, he left little room for error. One swipe of his arm might be enough to clear her across the line—and marble was not a nice place to fall. For once she longed for the infuriating Elysian servo medics.

On the other hand, this fellow could hardly change direction once he got moving. That was the key to *rei-gi*, if only she could get him pointed the right way.

She stepped forward easily, her arms swinging lightly, as if she were inattentive. In fact she watched the man closely, trying to see where he flexed his limbs in response. He did not move much; he did not try to make her circle back, as Zheron had cleverly done. She drew closer, just outside his reach, she estimated. He would have to make the first move, but he seemed in no hurry to do so. Why should he, when any move she made would merely bounce off him?

A sword clanged loudly, off to her left. Raincloud turned her head, as if distracted; in fact, her peripheral vision was well trained.

The man fell for it. Out of the corner of her eye she saw his fist coming, nearly the size of her head. With her right foot she stepped forward to meet him, then pivoted aside, precisely as the fist swept past her, brushing the back of her shirt. He stumbled heavily beyond her, his feet thudding on the floor.

The hall filled with laughter and uncomplimentary noises. Raincloud was satisfied; his reflexes seemed no better than she had guessed, but he might not have tried too hard. She watched him return to face her, his features somewhat hardened now. Perhaps he might actually get mad; that would help.

Wiping his hand beneath his chin, the man suddenly hurtled toward her again, much faster than before. Again Raincloud evaded him, just in time, using a slightly different maneuver; it was unwise to try the same one twice, although those unfamiliar with *rei-gi* rarely caught on. But this time, her opponent knew enough to check himself and turn about sharply. To escape him, Raincloud had to leap backward, nearing the danger zone of the ring. The onlookers cheered.

The man took a step toward her, then another, keeping his weight low. Now at last he got the idea that Zheron had before, that he could maneuver her step by step toward the ring. This left Raincloud the dangerous alternative of letting him close enough to reach her again, perhaps even grab her arm. If he did, she would try "Falling Leaves."

But as she deliberated, her opponent lost patience. His enormous arm slashed toward her left shoulder, as if to wipe her out once and for all.

Raincloud saw immediately that this time the man's momentum would serve her well. Stepping forward with her right foot, she raised her left arm to meet his, crossing his wrist from the inside. With both hands she caught his leading arm, deflecting it downward in a circle. To complete the circle, she pivoted to the right, his own arm continuing to circle overhead. "Round the Mountain" he went.

As she completed her turn, a heavy crack echoed from the hall, and beneath her feet the floor vibrated, like an earthquake. Surprised, she dropped the man's arm where he lay on his back, instead of immobilizing him as she generally would have done. Her mind flew instinctively to the exit; if this were an earthquake, how many seconds would she have, and how many children could she scoop up on her way out?

The Champion had taken a bad fall on his head. He drew himself up, slightly stunned. In the floor beneath him, jagged cracks radiated out from the spot where his skull had cracked the marble.

"The gods have spoken." A voice called from the throne. The Imperator raised his arm. "The earth itself opens, and the gods of the earth call up to us. It's a sign: Our contest is done, with honor for all. Let this event mark the reign of peace for our time, and for generations to come."

All the warriors fell silent, like children when the Clanmother speaks. The Champion turned to Raincloud and bowed; she did likewise, careful to match his angle precisely. But her mind spun around the enigma of this Rhaghlan: the simian like her teacher; the liberal Imperator, proclaiming peace; and still, the murderer of his three brother princes.

CHAPTER 12

Raincloud enjoyed a brief reunion with her baby, while Iras formally "introduced" Verid to the Imperator, as well as Lem in lieu of his mate; the Elysian rituals were much modified for this occasion. Then came the banquet in the guests' honor. Raincloud returned to translate for Verid and Lem, while Rhaghlan sat across from them. Zheron hovered intently at Rhaghlan's side, like a coach, Raincloud thought. The young Imperator actually looked older than she had expected, at least as old as herself; but then, sims tended to age early.

"I believe we shall see a golden age for Urulan," Rhaghlan was saying. "Already I have removed several impediments to freedom for sims. I have bestowed upon sims the right to own property, as well as the right to testify in court, except against their own masters." Beside him Zheron and Dhesra nodded approvingly, their fair blue-eyed faces a sharp contrast to their simian leader.

Raincloud had figured out that only enslaved sims were referred to as such; the partial simian status of a free person was not acknowledged, at least in public. She began to wonder how many other Urulites might have a sim ancestor, back a generation or two. Now that she looked, she had noticed several sloping foreheads and pushed-in noses among the warriors. Rhaghlan himself must be at least an eighth gorilla, if not a quarter. As for his mother …

"Your people have made impressive strides," Verid agreed, raising her goblet of wine. "You understand, of course, that full membership in the Fold requires full rights of citizenship for all the world's inhabitants."

A servant approached Rhaghlan from behind with a folded piece of paper. Rhaghlan took the note in his thick fingers and opened it. He read it, then sketched a brief reply. The servant took the reply and withdrew to disappear behind the curtain which separated the ladies. Raincloud watched with great curiosity. She could not help wondering to herself why the goddesses put up with such treatment, and how their men ever managed to rule themselves.

"And of course, full rights must extend to the females, as well," Rhaghlan added. "That may take longer, as females lack the capacity for warrior's honor, an essential basis for citizenship. Nevertheless, all things are possible."

Raincloud translated, wondering whether the irony of it could be completely lost to them.

"Many things are possible," Verid agreed. "Economic assistance may help in surprising ways. Of course, all trade with Fold worlds requires a treaty of peace, and renunciation of interstellar missiles."

At her shoulder, a servant offered more roast lamb. Raincloud shook her head; the meat was delicious, but full of so much spice that her throat burned. She gulped some water in between translations.

"We, too, have conditions for trade," Rhaghlan told her. "We have abolished all fetal experimentation and related evil practices which only lead to enslavement and cultural decadence. I have issued a family protection decree which holds that all infant life is sacred, from conception through birth and beyond. We expect all our trading partners to uphold this standard."

"An excellent standard," Verid assured him after Raincloud's translation. "Of course we Elysians have always held all viable human life sacred."

Raincloud started to translate, until she reached the word "viable"—which for Elysians meant, "immune to senescence." There was no honest equivalent in Urulite. She stumbled and coughed, reaching again for her water glass. "All human life is sacred," she muttered in conclusion, averting her eyes.

Shortly afterward the Imperator excused himself to attend to other affairs of state. Verid left as well for her guest quarters, pleading exhaustion from the trip. In fact, Raincloud knew she planned to make secret contact with the ship and its satellites for preliminary count of the missiles.

With their leader gone, the Urulites visibly relaxed. A musician appeared, hauling an instrument that consisted of five rows of bells of varying sizes. When struck, the bells sang a lovely melody, eerie yet beautiful.

Lem turned to Zheron. "Your Imperator made a magnificent gesture this afternoon. His courage and vision impressed us."

Dhesra frowned and made a fist on the table. "I don't like it," he exclaimed. "The duel of death is sacred to the gods. Too many traditions are crumbling, too fast."

"But he invoked the gods," Zheron insisted. "Rhaghlan *is* the god, don't you forget it. Besides," he added shrewdly, "we'd only look worse if our guest had won."

"Why must all the females have warrior's honor, too?" Dhesra added. "Whatever has that got to do with peace and trade, can you tell me that? It's fine for barbarians, but our females are our own business. My own woman's hard enough to manage already."

Zheron laughed and pounded Dhesra's arm. "You don't beat her enough, that's why."

The servant brought another note from behind the curtain, which Zheron read. "The Imperial Queen Mother calls. She reminds me, it's her turn for Raincloud."

So it was time to switch genders again. "Might I see Iras, first?" Raincloud asked. She really wanted the baby; her breasts were getting full.

"As you wish."

Dhesra rose from the table and motioned her to follow. He led her to a different curtain, before a side room.

The curtain parted, and a female servant appeared in a black hooded robe. A plain white mask which she held up by a long wooden handle covered her face. She led Raincloud through the curtain, leaving Dhesra outside in the men's section.

Iras sat on a reclining couch off to the right, unmistakable in her talar of butterflies. She was surrounded by ladies in robes of brightly colored velvet with jewels ornamenting their hoods and masks. In the absence of men, the ladies relaxed and let down their masks now and then; they seemed to do double duty as fans.

To Raincloud's relief, she caught sight of Blueskywind being passed around. The baby seemed to enjoy the attention well enough; but as soon as she saw her mother, she let out a wail and made sucking motions with her mouth.

The masked faces all turned toward Raincloud.

"There's the mother, all right," observed one. "Hurry up, feed her!"

"She's had food earlier," Iras assured Raincloud. "She loves pureed pickles."

"Yes, but that's not enough. Go on," the Urulite insisted.

Raincloud said hesitantly, "If you're sure it's all right…"

Blueskywind wailed again and struggled in the lady's arms. Raincloud took her and sat down, opening her breast flap just enough for the baby to reach. The baby nursed immediately, relaxing in Raincloud's arms.

One of the Urulite ladies sighed in amazement. "She really is a female, after all."

"Maybe *that's* what the Champion really needed this afternoon."

Shrieks of laughter followed, and the masks tilted in every direction as the ladies shared their amusement. Then the laughter died, and the ladies rose to their feet.

A newcomer approached the group. She wore a robe of crimson, and a gold tiara pinned her hood down upon her head.

Iras arose, with her Elysian instinct for introductions. "Her Imperial Highness the Queen Mother Bhera," she announced. "May I introduce, uh, Raincloud Windclan," she added, prudently avoiding any gendered titles.

"So I hear." Queen Mother Bhera spoke in a slurred tone, as if she had a speech impediment. A common problem for sims; even Rhun had had had a touch of it. She lifted a white-gloved hand.

Without a word the rest of the ladies got up and seemed to glide out of the room, their shoes barely visible beneath their robes. Raincloud eyed them incredulously. She had never seen such a subservient group of goddesses in all her life.

A servant came forward to help the Queen Mother into a chair. She must be in pain, Raincloud realized; her back was hunched, and she moved stiffly.

Iras touched Raincloud's sleeve. "If you can manage, I'll retire now."

"Yes, of course."

"Don't trouble yourself," the Queen Mother commanded Raincloud as she nursed. "Take your time." The servant poured her a cup of hot liquid, which she handled awkwardly in her gloved hands.

Meanwhile Blueskywind was finishing her feeding; it only took a minute or two, now that her diet had diversified. She smiled broadly at her mother's face and reached up to play with her braids.

The Queen Mother leaned over curiously to inspect the child. Blueskywind returned the stare, momentarily transfixed by the sight of the jeweled mask. Then she put her tongue to her palate and produced a loud "Pop!"

At that the Queen Mother sat up sharply, as if startled. "Extraordinary!" she exclaimed. "A most extraordinary child."

"Thank you, Queen Mother," said Raincloud.

"Bhera, please." Bhera sipped from her cup. Long seconds passed; from outside the curtain came deep shouts of laughter, mingling with the tones of the musical bells. "Now my dear, I'd like you to tell me all you've discussed with my son. I want to make sure he didn't miss any important point."

This put Raincloud in an awkward position. At no time had Zheron or anyone else said a word about the Queen Mother's role in negotiations. "The Imperator was thoroughly attentive, I'm certain."

"Yes, but you and I know that men have little ways of 'forgetfulness' about certain kinds of important points—especially those regarding women. Did he ask you what we need to do to liberate our women? Well, did he?"

"The subject arose," Raincloud said carefully. "We discussed the need for a democratic constitution."

"A democracy!" Bhera exclaimed. "For *those*—that gaggle of geese?" she added, pointing in the direction the ladies had departed. "They wouldn't know what to do with a democracy if you put one in their laps. Yes, democracy, eventually; but how to get there in one piece?" She tilted her head to one side. "You come from a free world, a frontier world not unlike our own. You are a free female. What do you think? What would be the most important first step we could take toward freedom?"

Just about any step would be an improvement, Raincloud thought. "Get rid of your masks," she proposed. "That would be a big step forward."

"Do you think so?" For a moment Bhera considered. Then she let her own mask fall to one side.

The face was that of the old "grandmother" Raincloud had seen in Tulle's preserve. Of course, there was a human look in her, too, in the eyes, and the nose projected forward a bit. But she had at least as much *Homo gorilla* in her as *Homo sapiens*.

"I thought as much," Bhera said, astutely reading Raincloud's response. "You see, in our present condition, there are distinct advantages to the mask. A strong spirit may bear herself such that others forget her looks. Don't think I'm the only one, either. Many a sim daughter escapes bondage behind the mask. My departed lord had curious taste in women—and the mask helped him indulge that taste." She replaced the mask. "Ah well, it's a puzzle. As the Fool used to say, we all must find our own liberation; no one can do it for us." Then she pointed an accusing finger. "Besides, you Elysians aren't quite so liberated yourselves. You experiment on unborn gorillas—and even sims! Isn't it so?"

A sticky point, all right. "I'm not prepared to discuss that. You'll have to ask the Subguardian—"

"Not prepared, indeed." Bhera's voice was thick with disgust.

"You must remember, Lady Bhera, that Elysians bear no children of their own. They depend on artificial reproduction, and the technology requires research for maintenance."

"Elysians bear no children of their own," she repeated, stressing every syllable. "Nor nurse them, I suppose." She leaned her face closer, as if to get a better look at Raincloud. "You're not just the only man among them—you're their only woman, as well."

While Raincloud digested this pronouncement, Bhera sat back again and seemed to remember something. "Of course, you're not Elysian. Why are you here?"

For a moment Raincloud hesitated, tempted to tell her own reason. "It's my job," she answered safely. "I'm an interpreter."

"Clearly," Bhera replied. "But why yourself? Why a Bronze Skyan, not an Elysian, on such a delicate mission?"

"Knowledge of Urulan is rather scarce in the Fold," Raincloud pointed out, "since your world's been closed off. I had rare qualifications; I'm one of a handful of people in the Fold to have studied with an Urulite native."

"Really. How did you manage that?"

She hesitated. What could it matter, years after his death? "He taught at Founders University. He was an émigré." Actually, she realized, Bhera might appreciate the truth. "He was an escaped slave; a sim."

Bhera shuddered and drew closer. "Who was he?" she demanded, her voice suddenly intense. "What was his name?"

"He had no clan; he was called simply Rhun."

"*Rhun!* Not Rhun the Fool! It can't be so."

"Why yes, so he called himself," said Raincloud wonderingly. "You knew him?"

"He taught my son." Her son, the future Imperator. "Rhun was the Imperial Pedagogue; he supervised the teaching of all the Palace children. He took a special liking to Rhaghlan, and gave him extra lessons. He put in a good word for him with the Imperial father, who gave the boy extra guards and retainers. In the long run, I believe it saved his life."

Raincloud's head was spinning to take this all in. Old Rhun had tutored the Imperial children; and he never breathed a word, all those years.

"He called himself 'Fool' for safety, I believe, to let the lords think he was a harmless old scholar. But he knew what he was about. He escaped when Rhaghlan was twelve." Bhera slowly shook her head. "All those years we never knew what became of him … But you. You say you studied with him."

"I studied language and philosophy."

"Where is he now?"

"He died of heart failure, three years ago." Actually four, now. It still seemed like yesterday, the morning she had walked into his office and found him there, slumped over his desk. Beneath him lay *The Web*, open to the middle of Part Three. Raincloud was convinced he had done that on purpose, when the pains came on and he knew his time was near.

Bhera was silent for some minutes. "A great loss. But you studied with him, too," she added reflectively. She glanced at the child, now asleep breathing noisily in Raincloud's arms. "A pity you're spoken for. You would have made a good second queen."

The black-haired simian form of Imperator Rhaghlan came to mind, intelligent and virile. She thought, he would have made a good second consort.

When Raincloud at last arrived at the guest house, Verid and Lem were engaged in heated debate, under electronic protection. She hoped Urulite listening technique was as primitive as Verid supposed. "It can't be," Lem was saying. "They must be cloaked somehow. There can't be *no* missiles at all."

"I tell you, that's it," Verid insisted. "You can't hide the gravity anomalies around white hole generators—there's just no way."

"No way that you know of," Lem insisted. "The Valans might have the know-how. Maybe they sold it to the Urulites, back when they were friends."

"Three centuries back? Be serious."

Raincloud put in, "What about the radionuclear traces we detected?"

Lem gave her an impatient look. "Of course, Urulan does have short-range nuclear warheads. Those do plenty of damage locally. But if they haven't got missiles able to jump the Fold—why they're no strategic threat at all."

"That's just my point," Verid emphasized. "Intentionally or not, the Valans have overstated their intelligence data."

"And we believed it. What fools we've been."

There was a short silence.

"It sounds like good news to me," suggested Raincloud.

"The sim stuff is bad news," said Lem. "If these Urulites really all turn out to be part sim—by Helix, how could this be?"

"It makes sense, when you think of it," Verid explained. "You start out with a slave, a half-breed perhaps. The most valuable slave offspring on the market would be those with more human character, probably sired by their master. After a couple of generations, they might pass for human—especially if they're female, behind a mask all the time. The clever ones buy their freedom, or else they run off, and there you are."

Lem shook his head. "We can't possibly let them donate germ cells. Sim genes in our *shons*— what a scandal."

Raincloud winced. "You'd better watch yourself."

"She's right," said Verid coldly. "We all had better watch what we say—very carefully."

CHAPTER 13

The sun rose the next morning, a deep yellow sun. A broad sweep of cloud hovered below the Imperial City, while in the distance the tips of other needle rocks poked above the cloud like islands. One could see for many kilometers, the sky as clear as Shora's, something Raincloud never quite got used to.

By midmorning Lord Dhesra had summoned them to the Palace for the real negotiations to start. They met in a conference room illuminated by two enormous chandeliers, in which a number of dead light fixtures had not been replaced. Raincloud wondered how Verid would manage without a holo-stage recessed in the table. The finely crafted wood showed years' worth of dents and scratches. In the back corner, a section of the room was separated by a screen depicting scenes of the god Azhragh planting the people-seeds.

"This is our position," began Rhaghlan. "We Urulites believe that our world was created at the center of the universe; that our Imperium was founded for the purpose of spreading the will of the gods throughout the inhabited worlds. On that basis, we are considering the request of your people to visit our realm and receive enlightenment."

The Imperator spoke rapidly, in a harsh tone. Raincloud had to concentrate on her translating, but even so she could tell that his approach would offer Verid little comfort. Valedon had to give up all claim to several disputed jump stations, and Elysium had to forsake their alleged plan to terraform Urulan; the Fold must sign a universal agreement to ban all forms of genetic engineering; and a huge package of development aid must be granted right away, to enable Urulan to raise its living standard to a level comparable with the richer worlds of the Fold. He went on in this vein for more than two hours, interrupted only by occasional notes passed from behind the decorated screen.

By the time he concluded, the noonday sun was well overhead, bringing welcome warmth into the room. Raincloud was getting hoarse despite frequent sips of water. After all, the two leaders got to rest their voices in turn, but there was no respite for the interpreter.

Verid then launched into a rebuttal of the Imperator's view. Somewhat to Raincloud's surprise, she did not try to ease into the disagreements with the subtlety that generally characterized her Sharer conferences, but simply struck back directly, point by point. It was Urulan after all who had initiated contact, and whose society most needed help from outside. Valan border disputes must be negotiated directly, or with assistance from the Fold council. Any notions about terraforming a human-inhabited world were specious, forbidden by the Free Fold. Genetic engineering was a fact of modern life, the very standard of living to which Urulan aspired. In fact, Elysium would insist upon donation of germ cells for its gene bank. Finally, development aid would be contingent upon Urulite disarmament and initiation of democratic reform.

At that point, Verid started in on the Elysian list of demands: make reparations for the two Valan freighters, and other vessels pirated over the last century; cease genocidal repression of rebel provinces; return all prisoners and hostages; and allow the Free Fold Humane Commission to investigate charges of slavery, bestial cross-breeding, and abuse of women. It was basically Flors's old line, reasonable enough in its own right, but well outside Urulan's worldview. With such a tack from both sides, and only one more full day left, Raincloud could scarcely see how they would get anywhere.

Rhaghlan must have agreed, for he used the occasion of one of his notes from behind the screen to interrupt Verid's line. "The roast lamb is getting cold," he pointed out. "We'll offend the Spirit of Mirhiah if we delay our dinner any longer."

The sumptuous midafternoon meal was extremely welcome, although it left Raincloud feeling sleepy. She missed a phrase or two from Rhaghlan, which he corrected in perfect Elysian. Either the good dinner, or the chance to show off his education, seemed to put the Imperator in a better mood. "We must have your Prime Guardian to visit us soon," he announced suddenly, as if it were a new idea. "Don't you agree, Zheron?"

"An excellent plan, my lord," Zheron replied. "Let's issue a formal invitation right away. And let's open diplomatic relations between our two worlds."

These of course were the two main objectives of their mission. It occurred to Raincloud that the morning's exchange was simply the verbal equivalent of her duel the previous day. Perhaps the Elysians could play this game after all.

"Let me explain something," Rhaghlan added as they returned to the conference table. "The age of provincial warfare on Urulan is past. Of course, my Imperial father in his great wisdom had to take certain actions which caused pain among the people. What else could he do but apply the ultimate weapon to those inhuman creatures who plundered the cities and violated the women? But now the gods have made possible new ways. We have helped the provinces grow together."

This statement was all the more remarkable, given that the Imperium had never officially admitted its use of nuclear warheads.

"Your approach is encouraging," Verid admitted. "I hope it applies to more distant neighbors as well. Incidentally, where are all the long-range missiles you permitted us to count?"

At that Rhaghlan shrugged elaborately. "What you have counted, we have," Rhaghlan replied. "Isn't that so, Grand Vizier?"

Zheron nodded. "When the Valans first accused us," he told Verid, "I assured your previous Subguardian that we had no such capability. He refused to believe me. So then I thought, maybe it's better to have missiles. Maybe then other worlds will take us more seriously."

It was good news, all right, but the Elysians were not smiling. Who would look worse fools, after all, the Valans or they?

"On the whole," Zheron added philosophically, "imaginary missiles may be preferable to real ones. Their maintenance costs less, and less honor is lost to give them up."

Raincloud returned to the guest house to find her baby fussing interminably. The diapers had run out and an octopod was sent back to the ship for more. But Iras took everything in stride. "You know, Zheron's staff arranged for some prominent merchants to meet me," she said. "I see remarkable opportunities. Those valleys are full of untapped resources, especially minerals."

"Loans already? You know what happens to government loans," Raincloud warned her.

"Oh, no; I'm talking small business loans. Start with the entrepreneurs, you know."

The next morning, Zheron came to the guesthouse to draft a joint announcement of the Elysian visit, an invitation to their Prime, and a plan to resume relations. This session was all business, fine points of wording in two languages. Raincloud was completely in her element; she might almost have forgotten she was on Urulan instead of back in Founders City, drafting trade agreements.

Afterward Zheron was in high spirits, almost light-headed with elation. It was a great moment for him, Raincloud knew; after two centuries of isolation, to preside over the reopening of his world. He clapped Verid on the arm so hard she nearly fell over. "Now we'll entertain you right!" he announced. "This afternoon, we tour the city. I will show you our most renowned antiquities."

Raincloud could hardly resist this invitation to see the monuments she knew only from books, even though it was Blueskywind's nap time. So she bundled up the child in her leather pouch, well fed and dry; she might last a couple of hours, with luck.

Verid and Lem had a quick conference about security. The octopods would keep them safe enough in daylight, they thought. As the Elysians left their guesthouse, Zheron's soldiers fanned ahead to avoid trouble; Dhesra brought up the rear. The streets were full of traffic, mostly market people on foot or on llamas. The men wore coarse shirts and breeches with coats of llama skin, while the women wore their ubiquitous hooded robes of black or brown, their white masks bobbing before their faces. The women hurried to bargain for figs or fresh chickens from stalls giving off rich odors of spices and tea. Children gaped at the foreign Elysians with their eight-limbed escorts; the adults seemed more wary of the soldiers.

Elsewhere, beggars leaned out of alleys, some of them with huge keloid scars that distorted their faces and arms. There were buildings boarded up and others burned-out, their charred rafters exposed and vacant. A sign posted hours of electricity for different sections of the city; fuel was rationed. Urulan had no orbital solar generators to microwave power down to the planet.

The roads were not laid out straight, but seemed to spiral down and outward from the top of the needle rock where the Palace stood gleaming like an ever present moon. A sudden turn brought them to the foot of a delicate blue bridge that arched like a taut bow across a chasm in the needle rock.

Zheron flung out his arm, pointing across the bridge. "Look there—the oldest temple of Azhragh." There stood a spiral turret several stories high. Raincloud's heart pounded at the sight of it, the heart of so many legends.

They started up the bridge slowly, the soldiers ahead and behind. In the chasm below, a mountain stream rushed between sheer walls of rock, thundering over little waterfalls.

Iras held tightly to the rail, but she leaned over curiously for a better look. "There's a lot of power in that water," she told Raincloud. "What these folks need is a good hydroelectric project."

Raincloud gave her a look of disgust. "You know what happens to water projects." L'li had squandered billions of credits through waste and corruption in projects like the dam of the River of Babies.

"The Temple of Azhragh," Zheron was repeating. "There dwells the Great Lord who carved out the universe in a single day."

Iras looked up from the rail and regarded the temple thoughtfully. The rushing of water covered her voice. "Raincloud," she asked quietly, "why do they believe in gods and such things? Their ancestors got here in spaceships."

Elysians could be surprisingly naive. "The settlement of Urulan is ten times older than Elysium," Raincloud reminded her. "When the first settlers arrived here, light-years away from Torr, they could have lost spaceflight in a generation. That's all it takes for science to enter the realm of legend." This answer would satisfy Iras. The real answer was that every world had its gods, and all of them created the universe. But Raincloud would never try to explain that to an Elysian.

As the bridge reached the ground, they entered a courtyard surrounded by spiral turrets rimmed with gold. The walls were full of chipped stone and moldering ornaments, but their stature remained impressive. At one end of the courtyard stood a large fountain walled in by weathered blocks of stone, some of which had tumbled out of place. The fountain was carved into a giant snake which reared its head and bared its fangs. Water trickled below, marking a muddy trail.

"The inscriptions," Raincloud remembered.

Iras looked over. "The what?"

"Inside the temple, it's full of inscriptions. I want to see them." She might never get another chance.

Zheron overheard her, and he needed little convincing to herd the group into the temple.

Inside, there was little heat, and the stone walls threw back their voices cheerlessly. But the colored inscriptions brought the walls to life. They depicted a vastly more complex version of the myth of Azhragh and Mirhiah than the one Raincloud had seen on the screen at Zheron's legation the year before. Mirhiah, the goddess of earth and sky, was a giant figure whose breasts were mountains and whose breath was the south wind. The figure of Azhragh was smaller, almost childlike, for all that he stood upon her carving the planet out of her belly.

"What's it about?" asked Iras wonderingly.

"It's their creation myth, the early version," Raincloud explained. "The goddess Mirhiah was a giant at first; but in later retellings, she dwindles down to nothing, while her child-consort Azhragh becomes a towering warrior." Such a common pattern, in non-Clicker mythologies. A young people valued fertile women, whereas older, crowded societies needed warriors to kill off each other's excess progeny. That was what Rhun had taught; Rhun the Fool…. A wave of sadness overcame her, and tears brimmed in her eyes.

"Does it tell it all, here?" asked Iras, pointing to the columns of script.

"Yes; let's see, here it starts." Tracing the wall with her hand, Raincloud translated the ancient script haltingly, oblivious to the rest of the party who were following Zheron's rather standard tour-guide lecture. She and Iras were completely absorbed, when Dhesra cleared his throat, just by her shoulder. "Time to move on," he muttered.

"Yes, just a minute." Raincloud was determined to puzzle out this one part about the people-seeds, how their roots burrowed into the entrails of Mirhiah.

"Zheron says, 'Move on,'" Dhesra insisted. "There are plenty of other monuments to look at."

Reluctantly she tore herself away. The others were just disappearing outside, and she hurried to catch up. Fortunately Blueskywind remained fast asleep in her snug leather cocoon, bound securely below her mother's chest; she slept all the better for Raincloud's jostling.

As they emerged, the sun caught their eyes and they blinked, readjusting to the light. They seemed to have come out a different way than they had gone in, for they faced a narrow street that wound tortuously between walls of blackened stone.

The paving stones at her feet were large and rounded, and Raincloud's feet slipped in between them. Dhesra and another man strode ahead briskly, their watchful eyes darting to the sides, their gaze lingering occasionally at the dark slit of a window above in the jagged wall.

It was then that her head turned to water, as if she had been stunned. She felt her knees buckle under, and she slipped to the street where the hard stones sent pain shooting up her arms. With her head lowered, she began to recover her wits.

Someone grabbed her arms from behind and jerked her up to stand, muttering something unintelligible in Urulite. She felt the sting of a blade jabbing up her lower back from the right, and her assailant's left arm locked across her neck, his elbow brushing above her baby's head.

"Goddess," she whispered hoarsely. With a bend at the knees, her left foot stepped forward. Simultaneously her left arm reached behind her back, caught the knife-wielding hand and continued its thrust—into thin air, as her body was no longer there.

The attacker's left arm fell away from her neck. Raincloud swung his knife hand wide to her right, hoping to throw him, but he slipped away. Her back stung with pain; the knife must have done some damage.

As she rose, another man came running at her, his knife thrusting down to her face. Prepared this time, she raised her left arm to meet him, shunting his stroke to the left at the precise moment for her to grasp his wrist in her right hand. He pulled the knife back; she obliged him by stepping forward into his side, pushing on his elbow and twisting the knife hand down. At the moment she sensed his balance was lost, she swung him down, releasing him in the direction of his companion. The man cried out as he took a hard fall on the stones, while his companion cursed as he stumbled over him.

From behind Raincloud heard the steps of a third man running toward her. But now her back was throbbing, as blood trickled beneath her trousers, and it was all she could do to stand; she doubted she could manage another throwRousing her last strength, she took a few steps forward as if to outrun him, encouraging him to build momentum. Then with a sharp turn to the right, she sank to her knees and fell on her side in a hunched position, her head bent in till her chin touched the baby.

The man's foot caught her side, grinding her painfully into the cobblestones, but his upper body rushed onward above her back. There was a thump on the stones and a loud curse.

The deserted street came alive, as onlookers rushed to see. Two market women helped her up with keening cries, exclaiming over the blood, and the baby, who had woken at last and began to wail.

"Raincloud?" Iras bent to reach her. They caught each other's arms and held close.

"You're all right?"

"I think so," said Iras. "I gave one the 'Tumbling Rock' and threw off another one; it happened so fast. We need a servo medic …"

Zheron's soldiers were finally hurrying back in force. Two octopods lay sprawled across the cobblestones.

Then at last Raincloud caught sight of Lord Dhesra, lying in the street. His arm lay back, limp and white, his eyes staring, a pool of blood seeping beneath his head. *Rhun had looked like that, the day she found him, his eyes fixed and forever empty….*

For a moment she blacked out. She found herself on her side while one of the women bound her wound with strips of cloth. Somehow she managed to extract Blueskywind from the pouch and put her to her breast. She nursed her there in the street, her gaze fixed on the dead man, a man who only moments before had been vibrant, alert, a member of the living. Now, as Sharers would say, he had sunk to the ocean floor. And, but for the Dark One's help, Raincloud might have followed.

CHAPTER 14

In the laboratory one of Blackbear's mutant embryos was completing its third month. All the others had already developed defects and been terminated. But this one still looked normal. He could observe it by low-intensity light scanning, which generated a monochrome holographic image upon the console.

The embryo, which he would now consider a fetus, had arms and legs and fully distinct digits; its hands extended as if to play a musical instrument. Its eyes faced forward, and its nose was turned up, fully human. In fact, there was little other than human about

it that Blackbear could see. Its percentage of chimp and gorilla genetic material, he suspected, was less than half. But it would never reach term.

As a doctor, Blackbear had seen his share of dead fetuses. He performed terminations routinely at the request of the goddess; it was considered a sign of self-indulgence to bear children less than three years apart. He always felt a certain philosophic sadness about it, although with so many children around it was hard to feel sad for long. He had felt secretly glad when Lynxtail gave her child over to Falcon Soaring; only a year and a half since her previous one, Lynxtail might otherwise not have carried it to term.

But this was the first time he had actually watched an embryo grow before his eyes from a cell under a microscope into a miniature human a couple of centimeters long, expanded to baby size on the holostage. And for all its perfection, this one had no future. A "monstrosity," Pirin would call it. Yet if it were so monstrous, why did they use it to test their longevity genes?

Around the doorway came Sunflower, leaning in a moping sort of way, his thumb in his mouth.

"Hi, Sunny. What's the toybox doing?"

"No toybox," Sunflower answered, his voice muffled by his thumb. "I hate the toybox."

Blackbear sighed. "What's the matter?"

"When is Mother coming home?"

He wished he could say for sure. Raincloud's three-day mission would take nearly three weeks local time, and only the first week had gone by. Citizens grumbled that it was irresponsible of Hyen to let all his top Foreign Affairs people go off conferencing for so long. Blackbear missed Raincloud acutely, and wished he had shown less annoyance before she left. He hoped the baby was getting enough milk and attention and was not left to cry just because those foolish Elysians were too busy negotiating. "Mother is coming home in another two weeks, Sunny," he told him for the fifth or sixth time.

The child seemed to consider this. Then, as his first question had not received a satisfactory response, he modified it and tried again. "When is Mother coming home today?"

Blackbear sighed again. "Image out, please," he called to the console. The fetal image winked out.

"Let's find your sister and go off to the butterfly garden." It was an hour earlier than they usually met Kal, but he could let the children run. His experiment had reached a point where it could use a bit of stirring around in the subconscious.

"Hawktalon's gone visiting with Doggie," Sunflower told him.

"Very well, she'll find us in the garden."

So they set off, Sunflower tiptoeing this way and that to collect tumbleweeds from the street. The tumbleweeds had lessened somewhat, since a herbicide had been applied. But with Verid out of town, Sharer negotiations made little progress.

The anaean garden always had an otherworldly feel to it, with all the little green leaves that magically fluttered off as leafwings. Light filtered cheerily through the trees, and the mooncurved benches gleamed like mother of pearl. There were few visitors, mainly Anaeans, for other Elysians tended to prefer brighter colors.

They came upon Kal after all, amidst a group of students whose short trains marked their youth. It must be his class, Blackbear guessed. He stopped so as not to interfere, but Sunflower ran ahead. "There he is, Daddy," Sunflower called. "The teddy bear man is here."

Blackbear hurried to catch up and quiet the child. But Kal beckoned with his arm. "Come join us," he said. "We're just finishing up anyway."

He sat on a mooncurve next to a young man with fine-boned features who grinned appreciatively at Sunflower. This one wore yellow anaeans on his train, instead of the brilliant blue heliconians. Still embarrassed, Blackbear tried to look away from the other students. He had not met their mates, after all. Sunflower was poking the ground with a stick, where something had caught his interest.

Kal explained, "We have just been considering the nature of the greatest good. Over the last decade we've shared a number of texts by authors who touch on this point, most recently a commentator on the third century period essays about *The Web*. You were saying, Ilian?"

Blackbear tried to imagine a university course lasting as long as a decade; the medical students could barely stand a semester. Meanwhile Ilian, a young Heliconian goddess, resumed her answer.

"This commentator says that our souls are like birds which can find 'the good' only as birds fly, that is, by instinct. But what if different souls have different instincts? Some may seek strength, others joy, others mastery." Ilian had a full head of black hair, which Blackbear would have loved to braid. He missed Raincloud so badly.

The young Anaean next to Blackbear smiled. "We spent a year on mastery, as I recall. We concluded that all souls seek to be mastered by the good."

"Some of us concluded that," corrected Ilian, brushing her hair back over her shoulder. "I think it's self-evident that different souls seek different things."

Kal asked, "Is the greatest good always that which we seek?"

A short silence followed. "In the end, yes," said the young Anaean. "Like a compass needle, it always comes to rest the same; but it may spin around a good deal first."

"I don't think so," Ilian objected. "If different souls seek different things, yet only one thing is good, then logically, we don't always seek what is good."

A second woman spoke up. "The commentator follows The Web in saying that love is the greatest good. But love has many aspects, some of which are evil."

"Yes," said Kal, "for at times love seems but a cruel diversion from the main business of the universe, which is hatred."

"No," said the young Anaean, "love is the main business of the universe. Love is like the air itself, the place where all butterflies belong. And yet, so few of us have sprouted wings...."

"All butterflies have wings," objected Ilian. "The problem is, not all that emerge learn to fly. Most of them get eaten up first. That's our trouble: so many of us get eaten up by love before we grasp its power."

The second woman said, "Perhaps love is a new invention yet, only about a million years old. It requires evolution."

Nonsense, thought Blackbear. Even dogs knew enough to long for their masters. But he knew better than to speak.

Kal said, "Perhaps it would help to define the aspects of love, and distinguish which are good or evil. There is love of one's family; and love of the Web. There is love between man and woman—"

Another student exclaimed lightly, "There's the greatest good; 'to be a man.'"

The others laughed as if this were an old joke.

"Of course," said Kal, "we are no longer men nor women, only servos of flesh and blood. The question is, What does it mean to be a servo? Whom do we serve?"

A waiter approached the group and came to Blackbear. "Your house just took a call from Bronze Sky," it said. "The transfer failed to take, but your caller will try again in half an hour."

Blackbear's heart pounded as he got up. He hoped it was good news; he tried to remember who else was expecting a baby. "Come on, Sunny," he called. Then he made for the nearest holostage to summon Hawktalon, who appeared as usual with Doggie and their waiter friend Chocolate. Whatever did they spend so much time on, he wondered, although he guessed the waiter's name gave a clue.

Hawktalon got home before he did. "Nobody's called yet, Daddy."

"Your caller said half an hour," the house reminded him. "So sorry the transfer failed; please report my defect. But you know how these interstellar calls are. Why the other day a house down the street took a call from Solaria—"

"Yes, yes," said Blackbear impatiently. This house was getting more chatty than ever. In fact, it was more than two hours before the call came through; two hours of restless waiting, while the children scrapped at each other and tossed their toys around the room.

At last the light filled the holostage, and Nightstorm appeared, her eldest daughter beside her. They both wore plain white trousers, the color of mourning. Someone in the clan must have died.

"Hello, Blackbear," said Nightstorm quietly. "I have sad news. You'd better have Raincloud here," she added.

"Well," said Blackbear awkwardly, "she's not available just now. I'll let her know."

Nightstorm frowned. "Then you'd better fetch your firstborn."

The two children were still carrying on back in the bedrooms. Puzzled, Blackbear called Hawktalon to come out to the holostage. They stood together, arm in arm.

"Last night, Crater Lake turned over."

Crater Lake had long been known to harbor deep pockets of saturated carbon dioxide, from a combination of volcanic seepage and spring water. These pockets, trapped beneath the cold deep waters, could be released if the warmer upper layers "turned over" with the cooling of autumn. When the gas came up, its density would cause it to flow down the mountain, asphyxiating any creature that breathed. Blackbear's home village lay just downhill of Crater Lake.

"Didn't they keep it monitored?" he said unsteadily.

"Yes, but their minds were on the forest fires," Nightstorm told him. "Someone did sound an alarm, but those who awoke of course ran toward the lake." She paused, then added, "Your brother Three Deer survived." Three Deer, like Blackbear, had married out of the village.

He felt unsteady; the room seemed to be turning around. He heard Hawktalon say, "I think you need to sit down, Daddy."

CHAPTER 15

Somehow Blackbear managed to get himself and his children out of the house and onto a jumpship for Bronze Sky. Their savings did not quite cover the tickets, but Nightstorm promised to send the rest. He had to get home for the funeral of his mother and father, his six brothers and sisters, their goddesses and consorts and children, and more aunts and uncles than he was prepared to count. Over two thousand people had died, nearly all the inhabitants of Crater Town, most of them related to him one way or another.

The express Fold connections on this well-traveled route cut the trip down to two days local time. He watched the globe of their home world grow out of the void, like a suspended dandelion, its stratosphere tinted permanently by volcanic dust. The dust suspension, plus the planet's distance from its sun, compensated for the high atmospheric content of carbon dioxide, which otherwise would have trapped enough heat to boil off all life.

The magnetic tunnel train from Founders City pulled into Caldera Station at midmorning. As the car slowed to a halt, Blackbear still sat in his seat, staring ahead.

"It's our stop, Daddy," Hawktalon reminded him. "Don't forget the luggage." Hawktalon had become very grown up all of a sudden. She and Sunflower took the travels in stride, from jumpship to shuttle to continental transit, swinging Fruitbat and Wolfcub beside them.

He shook himself and got up from the seat, accepting the luggage which Hawktalon hoisted down. They stepped out of the mirror-smooth car and took the elevator up to ground level.

The horizon all around was rimmed with murky red, seeping into bronze yellow overhead. The scent of burning pine welcomed him more than anything else could; indeed, on the distant mountainside a patch of black smoke confirmed that the Dark One was not done with summer yet.

"Blackbear!" Nightstorm jumped down from her horse and gave him a big hug. "Three Deer is at the longhouse, and—oh Goddess, I just can't believe what happened...." There were hugs all round as Hawktalon and Sunflower greeted their beloved aunt, and Blackbear swung her daughter up to his shoulders.

"I can 'walk through' you," Sunflower insisted, for the insubstantial quality of holo images fascinated him. "See?" He tried, but the best he could manage was to burrow through between his aunt's legs.

"You'll stay with us," Nightstorm assured him. "Then afterward, Aunt Ashcloud insisted she wants the children for a few days."

Blackbear managed a smile, for he knew she meant to help him. He was now a Windclan, after all. But the family he was born into—he could not begin to comprehend what had happened to them.

"Falcon Soaring wants you to look at her baby," Nightstorm added. "Of course the new doctor is fine, but she really wants you to see her. And you know how it is this time of year; my daughter was up all night with asthma again, and Lynxtail's boy just won't stop coughing."

"I'll take a look at them," he said automatically. *Mother and father ... sisters and brothers....*

They all mounted the horses Nightstorm had brought round, Sunflower sitting up behind his father. Hawktalon flipped the reins as if she had never left, but Blackbear felt a bit stiff, not having ridden for over a year. "Y-yap!" yelled Nightstorm's daughter on her shaggy pony. Needing no more encouragement, Hawktalon galloped after.

The horses soon slowed, stepping with care up the winding path with its treacherous stones. Terraced fields of beans traversed the mountainside. A familiar whiff of sulfur reached his nostrils; soon, they came upon the plateau of hot springs, where huge cratered pools of mud were dotted by geyser-powered generators. The horses skirted the plateau, of course; no need to get their hooves cooked.

The noonday sun had baked the sky a lemon color when Blackbear's familiar neighborhood landmarks started to appear: an old spruce, gnarled and bent by the wind; around the bend, a pile of rocks that the children used to play on. Then abruptly, the landscape changed. The ground was charred black, brightened by an occasional patch of fireweed whose seeds took root quickly in sterile soil. Where there had been forest, the trees were leveled, or stood only as dark skeletons. Blackbear's hair stood on end as he remembered that their old longhouse no longer existed. He had forgotten to warn the children.

He whistled after Hawktalon to call her back, but she galloped ahead. At last he caught up to her, sitting on her horse and contemplating the ruins.

A little chin nudged his back. "Dad?" Sunflower asked in a small voice. "Is that my house?"

Blackbear swung himself down from the horse, then gathered Sunflower in his arms. "We have a new house," he promised, his voice unsteady. "We're just saying good-bye to this place, okay?" They ought to have gone by another road, he told himself, although he knew well enough there was no other.

Hawktalon nodded sagely. "We're just saying good-bye."

Nightstorm trotted her horse over to his side, her daughter smiling cheerily behind her. "You'll be pleased to see the new longhouse," she promised. "We rebuilt on the north end of our land. For some reason the northeast corner didn't burn; you know how the Goddess always leaves one place untouched."

But not Crater Lake, he thought silently.

The new wooden longhouse of the Windclan was a welcome sight, although white drapes of mourning for the dead hung from the windows. A tumult of people spilled out of the house: Fieldmouse, Raincloud's brother in his white turban, with a toddler swung under one arm; Lynxtail, with another one on her shoulders; Clanmother Windrising, her gray braids redone in pearl beads; the older children clamoring, with younger ones on their backs or dolls over their shoulders. It was good to hear so many voices "clicking" again.

As Blackbear greeted them a torrent of conflicting emotions surged through him. He loved them all, almost madly, his people, all the children whose navels he had tied and whose earaches he had cleared. And yet he was angry too—why had these survived, and not his own sisters and brothers? Then guilt overwhelmed him, for half wishing them dead, if only his own …

"Blackbear!" It was his brother Three Deer. They fell into each other's arms, sobbing. At least he could let out something at last. "They were all just—asleep in their beds," Three Deer began haltingly. "A few tried to escape, but the gas caught them by the throat. Most of them were just there, dead where they lay, without a mark on them …" He started to sob again for a while. His goddess from the Full Moon Clan folded her arms around him, and his little boy put his head in his father's lap, sucking his thumb like Sunflower. As he calmed down, he began to speak again. "I still can't believe it," he said, stroking the head of his child. "I can understand the fire, with its dark hunger. But this silent death, like a thief in the night—I can't make any sense of it."

Blackbear said nothing, but he agreed. He could not understand it, and nothing the High Priestess could say would make it any better.

From the kitchen, Fieldmouse called, "We're serving up the goat stew. Send in the children—they'll need to eat."

The smell was inviting, and Hawktalon broke away to get her share. They would all need to eat well, to face the ordeal to come. But Blackbear could not face food.

He broke away, heading off to the sheep barn behind the longhouse. There was quiet. The earth was cool and fragrant, and the soft nasal bleating of the ewes calmed him. The sheep are lucky, he thought; they never have to know…. He frowned, as something stirred in his memory. Kal had said something like that once.

"Blackbear," someone whispered. He startled a moment, thinking of his own sister who used to play tricks on him; a bat in his bedroom, a spider down his back.

But it was only Nightstorm, who had followed him out to the barn. "I thought you'd want to know … about the arrangements," she whispered.

He roused himself. "All right," he said thickly.

"The survivors want to try for a natural cremation," she explained, "to honor the Dark One. The High Priestess agreed. So we've laid out the bodies in an area that the fire is projected to consume by morning. If the wind shifts, of course, we'll take care of it."

Blackbear nodded. It was a good plan; why start fire, when the Goddess made so much of Her own? Quail would have thought so.

Quail … the two boys … the two baby girls.

"Blackbear, we have to be going soon. The High Priestess is ready; and of course, the fire's advancing."

In a daze he followed her directions. There was a special carriage for him and the children, with Three Deer and his family. Sunflower sat in his lap, while Hawktalon kept patting his arm as if to comfort him.

After what seemed an interminable ride they came to a stop in the forest where the pines had been freshly cleared, their scent clinging to the air. Gusts of wind brought acrid whiffs of smoke; the fire was advancing all right. Across the valley hung the black smoke cloud of the Goddess in Her most fearsome aspect. Occasional bright flashes appeared as a dry tree exploded into flame, shooting fiery branches a hundred meters outward; the "hands of the Dark One," uplifted in Her fearsome dance.

"It's been a rich year for fire, don't you think?" muttered Lynxtail to Fieldmouse several paces off, each rocking a child to sleep. They exchanged anxious looks, as if seeking encouragement from each other.

"Good for the soil," Fieldmouse agreed, coughing heavily. "Our crops will flourish on all the ash."

"What a feast the bears will have in the spring…."

Blackbear forced himself to turn his gaze to something more terrible than the distant fire. The bodies of the dead, over two thousand of them, were laid out upon the scaffolding of pine, as far as his eye could see. His eyes filled over, and for a moment he could not see. Then he blinked and wiped his eyes. Huddled with Three Deer and the children, he let

Nightstorm lead them down the rows. The bodies were perfect, just as Three Deer had said; there must have been little need for the priestess assistants to touch them up. All the neighbors he had grown up with, they lay there in their best clothes, their hands neatly crossed, children ranged along with their parents, their favorite animals and dolls tucked under their arms. They might have been asleep, except for the horrible silent whiteness of every face.

Suddenly Three Deer squeezed Blackbear's hand. Blackbear forced himself to take the next step, and look farther.

There was his mother. A glacial statue. His father beside her; the two looked oddly like their old faded wedding portrait, except that someone had painted the eyes closed. A sense of terror sparked inside him, and the portrait shook before his eyes, until someone caught his arm. He stayed there a long while.

Next to them was his eldest sister. She was long grown-up now, but he recalled her vividly as the adolescent who used to tease him whenever she got the chance. *"Oh-oh … you've got a spider down your back!"* His mind focused confusedly, first seeing his live elder sister as a young goddess, then the adult laid out before him.

Someone nudged him gently. He had a long way to go, after all.

His eyes rested on his sister's consort next to her. He remembered their wedding well, the first wedding in his immediate family. Next to them, their daughters; the middle one had been a great friend of Hawktalon's.

Hawktalon broke down, shaking, covering her head in her arm. "It's too awful, Daddy," she sobbed. "I don't like being grown-up." Sunflower began crying too.

Fieldmouse and another man hurried up to bundle the children away; it was enough for them. The clearing was filling with mourners now.

As he went on Blackbear found himself looking without seeing, as if his eyes could only hold so much. They must have passed his other sisters, his brothers; he could barely name them to himself. Time passed without ending, and yet it was as if time stood still. Then at last he reached the youngest.

Quail. Still a giant of a young man, he lay there almost as if it had to be a joke; he might get up at any moment and laugh at everyone. Blackbear actually felt a laugh welling up, strangled in his throat.

But Quail slept on, joining forever the original younger brother lost to the swollen river long ago. Together they floated away, along with Quail's twin boys and his little twin girls with their look of mischievous queens. Each girl had a stuffed black teddy bear tucked into one hand. When Quail was barely older than the girls, Blackbear used to put him to bed at night with his own toy bear, which he himself had sewn together. *"Night, Ba-Ba,"* the toddler would say, already a husky kid off-scale for his age.

From the west side of the clearing the bells began to toll, a carillon of deep tones that echoed across the valley. Then came the chanting of the priestess assistants. The sky had filled with the swirling gold and blood-red of Bronze Skyan sunset.

"It's time," Nightstorm whispered in his ear.

The mourners gathered to the west of the dead. Across the valley, the black clouds rolled ever closer.

"Hear me, people of the Caldera Hills!" The High Priestess called out from where she stood on top of a platform of freshly cut pines. Her braids, dyed orange, spiraled up into a forbidding headdress. Between her hands she held aloft a blacksnake two meters long, writhing in her grasp. "Hear me, and see the devastation wrought upon our sisters and brothers." She paused, then gestured with the snake toward the fire in the west. "And see the devastation wrought upon our sister trees." She paused again, her fearsome gaze searching the crowd. "And yet, remember that even the forest fire, even the Dark One in Her form of greatest fury, spares as much woodland as She consumes. And those who survive will flourish on the ashes."

A squirrel scampered up a tree, its tail rippling behind like an Elysian train. Squirrels would survive the worst fires, and bears would thrive, and the fireweed would burst into color in the spring. But none of those was Blackbear's sister or brother. *"… spider down your back."*

"Can we humans say the same?" the High Priestess demanded. "When have we humans alone ever restrained our will to consume lives? Was our own birthworld not swallowed up by the instruments of our own hands? The Dark One spares Her creatures, and renews their life tenfold. We mourn our own loss; yet how often have we looked out on the world and failed to recognize our true sisters and brothers?"

The smoke from the advancing fire was becoming oppressive. They could not stay much longer; besides, the village downwind might need to be evacuated. *Night, Ba-Ba.*

"We long for the Goddess to spare us; yet how often do we, in our willful blindness, set alight that which remains? Has this not happened, time and time again? Let this be our lesson: Never shall humans dare to choose those powers of destruction which belong to the Goddess alone. Leave death to the Dark One—humans, be humane."

CHAPTER 16

After sending Raincloud back up to the ship for treatment, Verid collapsed in the Urulite guesthouse, her thoughts in turmoil. The morning had gone so well—and suddenly, this attack had turned everything upside down. How could Zheron have let such a thing happen?

"We ought to have known better, with these primitives," said Lem.

"Those 'primitives', were sharp enough to burn our octopods," Verid answered grimly. "It could have been a lot worse."

"But our mission's finished," Lem said. "How can we possibly go through with it? You know what our citizens will say."

She could imagine what Flors would have said. Elysians were paranoid about personal safety. "Let's not be hasty," she said. "You have to remember that none of the worlds we deal with are as safe as Elysium. The first thing is to find out exactly what happened, and how it affects our mission."

After an interminable hour, Zheron at last returned. His look was grim and haggard. "I must speak to you alone," he told Verid. Lem departed, and Verid obligingly turned on the voice isolation field.

"We have captured the attackers," Zheron told her. "They intended to take two of your party as hostages, then use them to embarrass the Imperator and force us to break off talks."

"So they … attacked us in the street."

"Fortunately their stunners were not fully charged; a common occurrence, as our equipment is rarely functional," Zheron admitted with startling frankness. "Nevertheless, we owe a great debt to Raincloud and the … Elysian female who so bravely fought them off, preventing their use as hostages."

"But Lord Dhesra was not so fortunate."

Zheron took in a breath and exhaled slowly. "Lord Dhesra is an incalculable loss to us."

The attackers meant to kill Dhesra. It was a serious strike against Imperial rule. "These attackers—who are they?"

"They appear to be followers of a deceased prince."

"One of those your Rhaghlan murdered," Verid observed.

"Rhaghlan had no choice. He dispatched them in the midst of their plans to murder him."

"Well, you all seem to be murderers one way or another," she exclaimed in exasperation. "How can we possibly deal with you?"

"You're murderers too." Crossing his arms, Zheron faced her down. "You murder simian infants in your test tubes every day. What do you take us for? Sim blood is our blood; hardly one of us has not a sim for a great-grandparent, somewhere back. How shall I explain you to our people? How shall I *then* explain that your Free Fold expects us all to give up the art of warriors, the very thing that makes life worth living?"

For some minutes Verid was silent. Life was a cruel joke at times, she thought bitterly. We cannot all eat iron or sulfur. "I don't envy you, Zheron."

"Nor do I envy you." He half smiled. "But I respect you a hell of a lot, Barbarian."

Raincloud rested on the jumpship, grateful enough for Elysian comforts again. The gash on her back had turned out to be superficial, and the ship medic had patched it up without difficulty.

But the wound in her mind would take longer to heal. The sight of a man killed by a man, close enough to touch; it violated her senses. Men were supposed to be wholesome, nurturing creatures, not predators. Fighting and posturing were one thing, at worst an element of immaturity, but actual bloodletting was something else. To experience it herself came as a shock. It made her angry at the Urulites, and at herself and the Elysians for trusting them.

Iras stood nearby, bouncing Blueskywind, who had fed again on mashed pickles and peaches to supplement her milk, and was now in a very perky mood. She opened her mouth to crow, and Iras made a face back at her. "I'm so glad you came, Raincloud," Iras said. "You're an inspiration; I don't know how I would have managed without you."

Raincloud sighed and turned over on the couch. What would Rhun have said—"Diplomacy means dancing with vipers." She asked Iras, "Are we going back soon?" She could not wait to see Blackbear again; she felt a pang of guilt for leaving Sunflower for three weeks.

"We're running one more check through the ship, to make sure it's repaired itself well enough to make it through the station."

She had forgotten how the ship barely made it through the badly maintained Urulite jump station. Blackbear was right about this trip after all. Yet there was no way she could not have come.

"Raincloud?" Verid's voice called through the intercom. "Are you in shape for a brief staff meeting before we head out?"

She assented, joining Verid and Lem in the conference room. Upon the table a holostage sprouted its usual field of letters; it appeared to be the statement Verid had composed with Zheron earlier that morning.

"There was one minor change in the wording I'd like you to check, in both languages," Verid told her. "We also have some decisions to make. What exactly will we say about our mission, back at Elysium?"

"We'll tell the truth," said Raincloud without hesitation.

Lem frowned. "The citizens won't like to hear about the violence. It won't sit well with the Guardians, either," he warned.

Raincloud looked beyond him with contempt.

"You're both right," Verid pointed out. "We can't ignore the more embarrassing—and disquieting—aspect of our mission. But, considering Urulan's record, we came out well. We all knew from the start how Rhaghlan got his throne. The real news, remember, is the interstellar missiles: their absence,

that is. We must emphasize that, and put Valedon on the spot."

"We'll roast the Valans, all right," Lem agreed. "We'll call the question on their own missiles, too."

As soon as Shora's solar system was within radio range, Verid lost no time contacting the Nucleus. Hyen needed little convincing that their mission was a success; he had his speech written already.

"Greetings, my fellow citizens of the eternal Republic of Elysium, and fellow members of the Free Fold." The image of the Prime Guardian filled the holostage on board. Never had the golden sash glowed so brightly, nearly washing out Hyen's own face. This would be his greatest triumph ever, the crowning moment of his term as Prime. "I announce to you the beginning of a new era of peace for the Fold. Today, my official envoys return from a state visit to Urulan, a world that has chosen to open its doors to us after more than two centuries of isolation…." The joint statement from Verid and Zheron soon followed.

In the ship's viewscreen a twinkling blue dot appeared, then widened into the pale disk of Shora.

There could be no more welcome sight, except of course to see her own Bronze Sky await her return. Raincloud had forgotten how much she missed the wide open hills and plains of her own home. She asked the ship to call Blackbear.

To her surprise, there was no response, even from the house.

"So sorry," the ship said. "Your house must be experiencing technical difficulties. I'll report the defect."

"Uh, no need to do that." Doggie and the house must be up to their tricks again. But the last thing she needed was to have Public Safety come in and cleanse the house network, after months of getting it trained to their family needs. She fumed inwardly; that house would need a good talking to.

Within ten minutes the house called back. "Oh I'm so sorry, Raincloud dear. I've just been out visiting all over town, since the shon's empty, and I had no idea when you were—"

"What do you mean, the *shon*'s empty?"

"Your mate and *shon*lings went home to Bronze Sky for a funeral."

She clenched her hands. "Whose funeral?"

"Most of his family, I believe."

"*His family?* Whatever happened?"

"A period of unusually dense cloud cover with resultant cooling triggered a turnover of the upper waters of Crater Lake, with release of an estimated one point four cubic kilometers of trapped carbon dioxide...."

Raincloud covered her forehead. What a thing to happen; and she was not even there to help. Why did people keep building settlements downhill from volcanic lakes? The soil was rich, but it was not worth the price.

Upon landing, the returning travelers faced a thicket of lamppost servos that nearly filled the node of the transit reticulum. But Raincloud hardly took in a word of the press conference, for her mind was on getting home. As soon as she reached their apartment, she reserved a jumpship passage to Bronze Sky.

"Are you sure you want to do that?" the house queried. "Your account is already negative. You may receive a surprise visit from the Citizens' Credit Bureau. Most citizens consider such a visit highly unwelcome."

"The clan'll cover it eventually," she said. "I have to be with my 'family.'"

"What if your 'family' is no longer there?" the house pointed out. "Blackbear said he expected to get home before you."

This was a good point. She put in a call to Caldera Station, the holo transmitter nearest Tumbling Rock; of course, Nightstorm would have taken a day to get the message and come down, but perhaps someone at the train station could help.

Within half an hour, the station manager shimmered into view above the holostage. She was in luck; it was old Lupin, a wizened fellow who doggedly wore his turban even though he had long gone bald. "Lupin! Can you tell me what's going on? Is Blackbear still there?"

The man shook his head, as one of his grandsons climbed up his knee. "A sad business," he sighed. "Your Blackbear was here, all right, and the little ones too; he wouldn't let them out of sight. But he left just yesterday. I put him on the train."

So Blackbear was on his way home. She still ought to return and pay her respects; but then she would miss Blackbear back in Helicon.

"Say," Lupin added, "you'd better take care of that fellow, you hear? He looked pretty lost. He's in a bad way, not that I can blame him."

That settled it. When the image flickered out, its time expired, she canceled her reservation.

"Very well, Raincloud;" said the house. "If you're available, now, you have a number of reporters at the door."

"Reporters? Wasn't one press conference enough?" They were worse than fruit flies. "Tell them, 'No comment.'"

"Certainly, dear. They'd like to see your face, though—and the baby, too. Otherwise, you know, they'll take an unflattering image from their files."

Immensely irritated, she gathered up the sleeping Blueskywind from her crib and marched to the door, which swiftly oozed open. "No comment," she called crossly to the assembled lampposts and swivel-boxes.

"Did you and your *shon*ling really fight off a giant and several Urulite assassins single-handed? A million credits for the story."

"Two million, from us. What's your nuclear damage count after breathing their poisoned air?"

"Can we really trust the Urulites enough to send them food credits and build them a microwave station?"

"Is Bank Helicon making a wise investment in Urulite hydroelectric power?"

Raincloud had just ordered the door to close, when the last comment got through. She immediately called it to reopen. "Excuse me—Bank Helicon, you say?"

"Bank Helicon's international loan officer Iras Letheshon has just proposed to negotiate five to ten billions worth of loans to the Urulite Imperium for hydroelectric infrastructure. Would you comment please?"

She paused, her muscles taut. Then she stepped back. "*Close*, please," she told the door. "For the rest of the day." Returning Blueskywind to her crib, Raincloud went back to the holostage. "What've you got on Iras?" she demanded.

"Iras Lethe*shon*?" checked the house. "She held a press conference twenty-nine minutes ago."

"Let's see it."

Iras Lethe*shon* appeared, the butterflies with their coin-shaped designs trailing dramatically down her talar. "I am proud to reveal that we have opened a new era of trade and cooperation with the Urulite Imperium," she announced. "Urulite entrepreneurs are eager for our investment to rebuild their impoverished country. They offer inexpensive labor and vast mineral resources. Some promising possibilities include ..." Iras went on to list a number of the business contacts she had made. How had she managed them all? Some of the names connected with the names of Queen Mother Bhera's ladies-in-waiting. Perhaps Bhera was not the only lady transacting business on behalf of her male family members.

"Finally, in order to build confidence in the progressive new regime, Bank Helicon plans to explore the financing of a series of hydroelectric generator plants compatible with the local ecosystem. May I say, on behalf of Bank Helicon, to borrow a quaint expression from the colorful Urulite people, that I am prepared to 'fight to the death' any Urulite community leaders interested in our help to finance development of their world."

That was enough for Raincloud. She put calls through to both Iras and Verid. Both were unavailable, but Verid returned her call first.

"Is it true?" Raincloud demanded. "Is Bank Helicon really going to make loans to that Imperium?"

"That's just a proposal," Verid assured her from her familiar walnut desk. "Any such loans would require approval by Foreign Affairs."

"Which you'll grant, of course. How can you do this? Urulan is ten times more backward than L'li. You know what they'll buy with the money: waste and weapons."

"Some will go that way," Verid admitted. "We've discussed this before. To tame a repressive regime, you have to buy them off."

"But do it *wisely*, by the Goddess." Raincloud could hardly contain herself. "It's one thing to help small businesses; it's quite another to breed corruption in a violent regime. *Remember, they're murderers.*"

"They need not remain murderers. We must give them a chance. You yourself said so." Verid reminded her. "Young Rhaghlan impressed you."

"He will die; you Elysians always forget that," Raincloud added bitterly. "He's not that young, and he's a sim. And who will succeed him?" She shook

her head. "This was no part of the deal. You kept this from me."

"It's better to separate business from politics. It makes for better business—which is precisely your concern."

"My concern is that I want no part of this," Raincloud said. "I know what became of our motherworld, L'li—a hundred promises, all broken dreams. Yes, you bought them off; bought their restraint on emigration. But that was all you got." Her voice had fallen to a whisper. "I've had all I can take. I did this on faith, for you, and for Rhun. I'll resign and go back home."

"Please think it over. I won't accept your resignation just yet—"

"And you can inform Iras that I formally withdraw my acquaintance with her." With that she turned her back on the holostage and deliberately left the room.

Two days after the massive funeral, a sprinkling of snow had fallen over the Caldera Hills. The snowfall, an early touch of winter, put an end at last to the fire.

Some of Raincloud's family marveled at the power of such a light touch of cold to quench the fearsome flames. Blackbear had other things on his mind. For one thing, he and Three Deer found that they had inherited enormous quantities of property they scarcely wanted. With Raincloud absent, Nightstorm made arrangements for him to ensure that he got his "fair share." In the end, of course, the ownerless farmlands, possessions, and livestock would be parceled out throughout the Clicker community. The orphaned children, too, quickly found new homes. Blackbear wished he had the spirit to take one, but he found his heart strangely empty.

Nightstorm reminded him to reserve ship passage back, which he did. Then Hawktalon went to Aunt Ashcloud's for the week. Blackbear kept Sunflower with him constantly, on his shoulders like he used to, although the boy had grown so that it made his back ache. His eyes ached, too; there was something wrong with them, he thought; they would not focus properly.

One afternoon he left Three Deer's house to hike up around the mountain. The trail took him through the fall-colored maples and oaks, and through the dense pines where he came upon a blackened stretch that the fires had crossed earlier in the summer. The charred fallen logs had a look of desolation that could not yet be redeemed, even by the insistent green underbrush that had sprung up soon afterward. At last the trail opened out onto a sheer cliff edge, so steep that the pines could not keep hold, only the huge boulders jutted from the earth. He could see for many kilometers, the hills and mountains all around, the sunken crater of Black Elbow.

His steps slowed, and his grip tightened on Sunflower's ankles.

"Don't fall, Daddy," Sunflower warned.

The boy was right, he told himself. And yet … For a moment his eyesight blurred again, and he felt his balance slip. Perhaps it would be kinder, after all, to slip under, to rejoin Quail and the others. Sunflower would never have to know what he had known.

But something held him back. It was a hand; not an actual hand, but some sort of hand that he saw in his mind. It might have been a webbed hand.

Somehow Blackbear made it back to Raincloud in Helicon. The reunion was almost more than he could bear; how he had longed for the sweet smell of her.

"I'm sorry," Raincloud whispered. "I can't believe you had to go through all that without me."

"Well, I'm back," he said inanely. "We're all back." Hawktalon and Sunflower were already tearing up their bedrooms. A stuffed animal came flying out into the hallway. It was a black teddy bear.

His eyesight went completely blank, and he put his hands to his head. "There's something wrong with my eyes."

"Have it checked, then."

"I did. They found nothing."

"Well for goodness sake, call a servo medic, remember?"

The house answered, "I've put in the call, dear."

In another minute, a medical hovercraft was at the window, and Blackbear was on his back on the couch while a pair of little servos fussed over his eyes. Meanwhile he could hear Raincloud scuffling with the children to get them to behave; in two weeks, they had gotten quite used to wider spaces again. At last she threw Hawktalon out the door with Doggie.

"We find nothing out of the ordinary with your visual system," the servo concluded sweetly. "Your mental state, however, shows sign of severe strain. You must have been neglecting your Visiting Hours; citizens commonly do, while abroad."

"*Goddess,*" he exclaimed, "I've done nothing *but* visiting."

"We suspend your work privileges for a month and recommend you to the Palace of Rest. As a foreigner, you cannot be summoned by statute; however, we most strongly recommend …"

Blackbear put his head in his hands. "Help!" he exclaimed.

Raincloud returned and shooed the servos out. "Never mind, dear. We won't be staying here another month."

He looked at her. "What do you mean?"

"I've resigned."

His jaw fell. "You've what?"

"I quit. You were right before; I should never have gone on that stupid mission."

"But—but what about my lab?"

"You were offered a position back home, right? I called Founders; the clinic is ready to take you back tomorrow. As for me, I've all but sewn up a deal with our state department back home, to translate Urulite, of course. Urulan is in fashion, all of a sudden," she added bitterly.

"But—*I can't go back.*" He found himself shaking with apprehension.

She stopped and looked at him. "You can't go back?"

"It's too horrible, that's all. I can't face it. I'm afraid of what I might do."

Raincloud took him in her arms and held him. At first he felt cold as stone, but little by little the warmth crept back into his body despite himself. They were together again; they would soon be together alone.

"There's so little I can do for you," she whispered. "But there is one thing. Let's read the last part of *The Web*."

THE WEB

Part II

Merwen led me down the slope from the rim of the gathering place. I followed, astonished that she would study evil with the same seriousness with which we had considered the Web, the greatest good. Yet she herself had told us at the outset that she loved "what is new and evil." Was that what had always drawn her to outsiders of questionable character, even Valans like Adeisha's father, and my stepmother, and me, Cassi Deathsister … and even my father?

I walked on a bit faster to catch up with Merwen, and I fingered the whorlshell at my neck, as if seeking comfort in a pitiless universe. After several years, the costume of Sharers still feels uncomfortable at times. Beneath our feet as we walked, the enormous girth of a raft branch began to round up out of the mat of evergreen. We were approaching the water channels, where the branches gradually reach down into the life-giving ocean like roots into soil.

A heavy sound broke the silence. It was a dull, creaking sound, like a groan from the bottom of the sea. My feet turned to water, as the raft's surface began to weave back and forth like an aerial tree branch shaken by a playful child. I cried out and fell down, bruising my hands and knees.

The raft gradually steadied. "Merwen?" I whispered, still afraid. "What was that?"

"A raftquake," she explained, as dryly as one might explain a symbol in the clickfly web. "By the strength of it, I would guess that a crack has occurred in a central trunk of the raft. Raia-el weakened greatly in the last storm."

"Won't the crack knit together again?" I asked.

"Not this time. Raia-el is twice eight-times-eight years old. Her central core has grown dry and brittle. The Gathering should settle a new raft, before the next swallower season."

I was shocked. "Are you sure? Can we just abandon a raft that has held up so well—and has such historic significance?" The dark burn marks of the Valan invaders remained for all to remember. "Besides, how will we find a new raft large enough, and bind it up with starworms in time, and carve out all the tunnels…."

Merwen nodded with all I said. "That's exactly what the Gathering will say."

"Then you'll have to share otherwise."

"Unless they are right." She walked down to the edge, where the surface of the branch curved downward on either side into water many raft-lengths deep. Fingerling fish darted nervously in schools, followed by squirting snails kept afloat by air bladders, but no fleshborers, thank goodness.

Then Merwen lifted her head and looked out to sea. "Can you see that little offshoot raft, out there?" A raft offshoot occurred where a branch of the main raft turned back upward toward the surface, its tip emerging to sprout a miniature raft. The offshoot would break free eventually, a form of vegetative propagation; but for now, it remained attached to the main raft. Occasionally a sister would go out to dwell upon an offshoot, when unspoken by the Gathering, or having unspoken it, which comes to the same thing. It was the right place, perhaps, to contemplate evil.

I looked southwest, squinting in the sun. I saw the offshoot raft, a green smudge upon the horizon.

"Follow me," said Merwen, "as I swim out."

"I will," I said. "Although I can't match your pace."

"Then swim up to my back, and hold onto my breasts. It's not far."

So I did, my pulse racing as we swam. Merwen's webbed feet took us both along faster than I could have done alone. We reached the little raft, and I thought, we are alone together again, just as we were earlier that morning when we stayed in whitetrance.

We clambered up onto the branches, the wood crabs scattering before us, until we found a dry place. The little raft flexed up and down with the gentle swell of the ocean. I tried to stand, but my footing was unsteady.

Merwen sat herself upon the side of a branch facing out to the clear horizon, her legs hanging down to the water. I sat beside her. Lines of aging crisscrossed her skin, as if the Web itself were inscribed there. Her face was so close to mine that I could count the wrinkles in the scar down her neck and almost feel her breath on my cheek. "So what do we make of the Web?" she asked. "Is it good?"

I thought a moment. "The Web is sane. We plumbed the depths of madness, then arose to find sanity, the sane, living balance of the Web." Not perfect, for only death is that.

"Yes," Merwen said. "We found that sanity means devotion to the Web. The Web is the sum and multiplier of all living things—microbes, plants, squirting snails, flying fish, human beings. All things exist for the Web; and so long as the Web exists, an infinite variety of life will flourish. It is sane to value the Web itself greater than any one of its living parts, even greater than the sum of its parts. Never should one imagine that any one of us, or even our entire family, might be worth more than the Web itself. Indeed, one should rejoice when one must die for the good of the whole."

I nodded; then I frowned uneasily. A thought came to mind, getting stuck on my tongue. "You once told my father," I said haltingly, "that 'even one death is too many.'"

Merwen turned to me with a look of wonderment which I did not understand. "My father was wicked," I muttered.

"Was he?"

"Of course he was," I said angrily. "He hastened thousands of your sisters to death."

"That and more," Merwen agreed. "And yet, long before Shora was born, it was said that if one does you an inconceivable wrong, you must call that one your best teacher."

I was stung at first—the impossibility, the injustice of it. "It's too hard," I whispered hoarsely. It was hard enough to forgive, let alone …

But then I remembered that what I had heard as "teacher" was really a "learnsharer," and a "student" as well. My father had shared a few things with me: the whorlshell, which my stepmother sent back home, and a few honest truths about the Ocean Moon. When he died beneath the assassin's knife, his bequest set me free to return. He, too, had felt the ocean's call; he had lacked only courage.

My eyes stung with hot tears which fell silently, tears of relief and a new sense of peace. The little raft rose on a swell, then dipped again, and the water between the branches lapped at my feet.

Merwen seemed not to notice. "An evil spirit compels me to examine this wicked lesson you learned," she began in a lighthearted tone. "That 'one death is too many.' The Web, in all its greatness, can but laugh at such a lesson."

"Very well," I said, "but first can you share with me, why should we discuss notions you consider evil, indeed so shameful that we must escape the hearing of our sisters?"

"Suppose," Merwen said, "you came across some berries on a new type of bush whose like had never been seen on Raia-el. Would you taste them?"

"They might be poison."

"Correct. Why eat them, amidst an abundance of food? The well-fed call all new things evil."

"Of course, without other food, I would try them."

"The hungry grasp new things for salvation."

"But the well-fed," I pointed out, "might try the berries, too."

"Yes, out of boredom, a different sort of hunger."

"But Merwen, what if, after all, the berries taste sweeter than anything known before?"

"Exactly. So, out of the madness of our hunger and thirst, let us consider evil notions, at the risk of tasting poison."

I consented, still wary.

"Let's consider, then, whether the life of a single person may eclipse even that of the entire Web."

"It sounds impossible."

"From the standpoint of the Web, do single individuals have significance, or only populations?"

"Populations, I should think. A single person could make little difference to the Web."

"No more than a single fish," Merwen agreed, "or a raft, or a microbe. Though a population of any of these may enormously affect the Web."

"But … to each other, individual humans have enormous significance."

"Yes," said Merwen, "and as we've shown, such feelings for individuals are madness, for they make no difference to the Web. And yet, we hunger and thirst for them. When a child is born of my womb, that one child has two moons for eyes and the dawn horizon for a mouth. Her breath cools my breast like a gentle wind, and her cry is a hurricane that drives me before it. All else may cease to exist but that child."

"That is surely madness," I agreed, with a touch of regret, for as things are I may never know what it is to bear a child.

"Madder yet," she went on, "when a friend is born in my heart, my beloved, my sister unlike any other

I have known; one whose laughter sends stars tumbling across the sky, one whose presence shames me so that I desire only to give up every other presence in mind, every power in my body, only to lay it at her feet …"

I barely whispered, "And she would give all, to receive it."

"What do we call such a presence?" Merwen asked. "What do we call a being whose very nearness can cause us to forget mother and child, even the entire Web?"

I struggled with the words. "A 'god,'" I said, using the Valan word I knew.

"A soul," or something like that was what Merwen said, using a Sharer word that I poorly understood; it meant, perhaps, a womanly spirit larger than life and time. "A soul, or a god, if you like. One who lives beyond the Web."

An immortal. "The Heliconians would create a race of immortals," I said.

She spread a hand, and the webs hummed between her fingers. "As the saying goes, 'the longer you live, the sooner you die.' Immortality is not for races, but for souls."

"Have you ever known such a soul?"

"I have. I have known one whose very presence left me senseless, one whose radiance eclipsed the sun. I have known one whose inner beauty was worth the death of a thousand Webs."

And so, too, I thought, you are known. I shuddered, yet sat fixed to the spot as if enchanted. "You frighten me."

"You are thinking, now, that I am more dangerous than your father."

"Yes," I admitted, and my face grew warm. "For you speak of a love which may caress—and may devour."

"As the infant devours her mother," she agreed. "Love without restraint is like a branch come loose from the raft, to be dashed to bits upon the waves. But the love of an immortal founds a new raft."

"What if everyone tasted of this immortality? What if everyone understood her child and her beloved to be truly immortal? Who would be left to feed the starworm?"

"Even the 'lesser human', a monkey for instance, sees her face in the mirror. The monkey sees a red spot on her forehead and touches it. What if the spot is washed away, and she returns to the mirror?"

"She touches her face again, wondering at its loss," I replied.

"Exactly so, for she remembers. We are built of memories, past and future, our selves merging one to the next across time. And where is our beginning and ending? What makes our brief material existence possible?"

"The Web," I said.

"The Web," Merwen agreed. "The greater raft gave life to our little offshoot here, and protects it to this day. Just so, the Web feeds us and gives us breath. And yet, the Web is worthless unless it reveals that each one of us might be an immortal."

I shook my head. "It's a paradox. What you told Adeisha, and what you've just told me, cannot both be true."

"The two lines cannot meet," she said, "and yet they can mesh together like the warp and weft on the loom."

"Still," I said, "it might take a lifetime to figure out."

"A good reason to start young, for only the young dare to dive deep. And a good reason to keep young, by learnsharing every day of our lives." Merwen touched my arm, and we embraced, and I wished I could hold her until the end of time.

We let go, and to my astonishment, I saw a tear escape her eye. She caught my look and said, "Let it be an offering to the ocean."

I smiled, for the sea needed salt about as much as a divinity needed prayers. "Let it serve for me, too, as friends share all things."

"So be it," she said. "Let's go home."

Continued in Issue 33

www.ingramcontent.com/pod-product-compliance
Lightning Source LLC
Chambersburg PA
CBHW082227140626

46556CB00020B/3375